praise for
return to
Farrellville

Return to Farrellville is a return to family values. Young children learn best through stories. Gerald Brock understands that and creates Farrellville to entertain and to teach children how to be the best that they can be. In each chapter he develops a new character and a new lesson for young minds to absorb. Parents and grandparents everywhere will find *Return to Farrellville* a wonderful book that will make story time with their children a warm and magical moment.

—*Roberta L. Noonan*
Vice President, Bobbie Noonan Child Care
Principal, Noonan Elementary Academy

I had two of the top readers in my sixth grade class read *Return to Farrellville*. They both loved it and couldn't put it down. Each finished it in one day.

—*Theresa Schicitano*
Teacher

return to
Farrellville

M. E. Bond

return to
Farrellville

G. E. Brock

TATE PUBLISHING & *Enterprises*

Published by Tate Publishing & Enterprises, LLC
127 E. Trade Center Terrace | Mustang, Oklahoma 73064 USA
1.888.361.9473 | www.tatepublishing.com

Tate Publishing is committed to excellence in the publishing industry. The company reflects the philosophy established by the founders, based on Psalm 68:11,
"The Lord gave the word and great was the company of those who published it."

Book design copyright © 2009 by Tate Publishing, LLC. All rights reserved.
Cover design by Blake Brasor
Interior design by Stephanie Woloszyn

Published in the United States of America

ISBN: 978-1-61566-309-5
1. Fiction / Christian / Short Stories
2. Fiction / Family Life
09.10.20

dedication

*To Vern and Marge, Earl and Eva,
and Tim and Maude,*

who gave me values that I now hand down
to my children and grandchildren.

prologue

I returned to Farrellville this week after an extended absence. The call last week from my grandmother, telling me that Granddad Earl had died suddenly, brought me back. My work abroad had not allowed me to be here the past three years.

You see, Farrellville is where I spent many of the happiest moments of my childhood. Since my mother, an orphan, died when I was two years old, and my father, as a military man, traveled throughout the world for much of my youth, I spent extended periods with my paternal grandparents. Farrellville welcomed me and in many ways became my hometown because of my granddad, whose vision and resources were responsible for its establishment. He introduced me to its residents and their lives.

As I sit here in Granddad's house, following his funeral, I can recall my first visit to Farrellville and the people I met there.

daniel

Stop judging by mere appearances,
and make a right judgment.

John 7:24 (NIV)

Daniel was the first resident that Granddad introduced to me in Farrellville. Daniel always wore blue jeans, a bright red shirt, and an old-fashioned brown fedora. Daniel was, as the townspeople referred to him, "a little slow or simple." Although very friendly and good natured, as Daniel grew into adulthood, his diminishing memory resulted in him constantly finding himself in unfamiliar places in his own hometown. Thus, the townspeople were constantly watching out for him, and the most common daily question in Farrellville was, "Where's Daniel?"

As a child, Daniel was the butt of jokes from other kids his age. They would send him on wild goose chases under the guise of "errands." Wanting to be accepted by the gang, Daniel was anxious to please, and therefore, took each "mission" with deadly seriousness.

"Hey, Daniel, the principal wants you to take these bricks to his office," Jimmy Swatmore proclaimed as he loaded them into Daniel's backpack. Dutifully, Daniel trudged from the playground into the administration office and proudly announced, "I'm here with the bricks for Principal Schafer."

On another occasion, Willy Packard had Daniel deliver his lunch to the prettiest girl in the school, Sarah Farnsworth, on the premise that hers had been stolen from her locker during first period. Daniel's sincerity won Sarah over, and thereafter they became friends, much to the chagrin of Jimmy and Willy and their gang. As he grew older, Daniel's good nature won over most of the school.

Not much was ever expected of Daniel, especially by his teachers, but that didn't stop him from applying himself completely to any task given him. Daniel's father, always a little embarrassed by him, never gave him the encouragement to do more than the minimum. That was left to his mother, who was his biggest champion. "Effort and persistence can move mountains. Just look at the ant, the smallest of God's creatures," she told him over and over. It became his motto every day.

This was put to its greatest test when Daniel was eight and would change more lives than just his own. The day began as any other school day, with Daniel walking along the railroad tracks that ran near his home. Although walking on his street into town would have been quicker, Daniel preferred the tracks because the 7:40 a.m. local would pass him halfway to school. The conductor would often wave to him and swing his light as the train gained speed from its stop at the Farrellville station.

The smallest of occurrences can create great impacts. Such was the case earlier in the morning, when stones from the quarry train fell into the switch points as it moved from the siding onto the main track. These stones prevented the switch on the main track from closing tightly. As the 7:40 began to pick up speed, the engine's wheels hit the open switch, derailing the engine onto the adjacent road. Daniel, hearing the screech of the wheels as they derailed, turned just as the train jumped the tracks and headed for the road next to the train bed. The approaching school bus was in its path, and only the quick reaction of the bus driver prevented a collision. The quick turn of the wheel, however, drove the bus down a steep embankment, where it struck head-on a large tree at the riverbank. The bus listed to its side, the wheels spinning from the unconscious bus driver's foot on the accelerator. Gently sliding sideways in the soft soil of the riverbank, the wheels lost their purchase, and the bus tipped on its side and slid into the flowing water, killing the engine. The screams of the children were gradually being drowned out by water rushing into the broken windshield of the bus.

Initially shocked and then confused, Daniel understood that he needed to do something, and fast! Looking around, he could see nobody to turn to for help. So the "slow and simple" Daniel decided that it was up to him to help the kids in the bus. With adrenaline rushing into his system, he ran faster than any time in his life to the riverbank and jumped on the bus. The first person he saw was Sarah, who was pressing against the bus window. Other kids were doing the same, trying to stay above the water that was quickly rising. What could he do?

"Help, Daniel!" Sarah yelled. While he knew that breaking windows was not proper normally, he understood this to be a time when it was necessary. What could he use to smash the window? He looked around for something, anything! Finally, he saw some rocks on the riverbed about fifty feet up the river.

"Sarah!" he shouted, "I-I-I'm going to get a rock to break the window. I-I-I'll be right back!"

Running to the rocks seemed to take forever. His shoes sank in the soft mud on the riverbed. As his right shoe stuck, he ran out of it and stumbled forward, nearly falling into the water. Reaching the rocks, he had to decide which was big enough to smash the window. Most were clearly large enough, but were too heavy to carry back to the bus in time. Finally, he found two that he could carry in each hand, and ran back to the bus.

The water filled the bottom half of the bus, and the children were now all pressed against the upper windows. "Get away from the windows!" he yelled. Not wanting to back down into the rushing water, Sarah and Theresa, a girl in Daniel's class, climbed over the seat in front of them.

Daniel threw the rock in his right hand against the bus window and saw it shatter. As Sarah tried to climb through, the jagged edges sliced into her arms. As she cried out, Daniel shouted, "Get back, so I can break the points." With the rock in his left hand, he broke out the shards still held by the window frame.

"Give me your hand so I can pull you out!" Sarah reached for Daniel, who pulled her through the window. Daniel pulled out each child as they scrambled to the window. As he was reaching for the last boy, Daniel heard a voice behind him. "I'll get him, Daniel." It was Officer Rick Singer, who had just responded to the emergency call placed by the conductor on the train. Suddenly there were other men who were leading the children up the embankment to a fire truck and ambulance, where they were checked for injuries.

Standing aside on the riverbank, Daniel started to tremble and fell to his knees, shaking. With his adrenaline spent, he now felt weak and couldn't catch his breath. Officer Singer lifted Daniel, carried him up to the road, and set him in the patrol car. "You'll be okay, Daniel. You did a brave thing today."

"I-I-I didn't know what to do! I couldn't find anything to get them out. I lost my shoe in the river."

"You did the right thing, breaking the window with the rocks. You were very brave, Daniel." Then Daniel began to cry. He was embarrassed but couldn't stop.

Just then, Daniel's mom ran up. "Daniel, are you all right?"

"He's fine," Officer Singer said. "Your son's a hero today!"

"Mom, I lost my shoe in the river!" he cried.

"Don't worry about that now. Thank God you're safe!"

"How's Sarah?"

"She has some pretty bad cuts on her arms," Singer replied, "but I think she'll be all right. Thanks to you, Daniel. The other kids seem to be okay. Just bumps and bruises. The bus driver just left for the hospital in the ambulance, and it looked pretty serious."

Daniel looked back at the train. The engine had not tipped over but was straddling the narrow grass area between the rail bed and the road. The rest of the cars were still on the track. If the train had not stopped at the station and had been traveling at normal speed, the injuries and damage would have been disastrous. As it was, no one on the train was injured.

In the weeks that followed, Daniel would relive the school bus experience in his dreams, hearing the screech of the locomotive's wheels, the collision of the bus with the tree, and the screaming of the children. Over and over, he could see Sarah's face through the window, calling for help. His run down the riverbank to retrieve the rocks would seem to be in slow motion. He could never get there. In other dreams, he would be throwing the rocks at the window with no effect. They would bounce off the glass. He would pick them up and throw again. Each time, he would wake with a shout, out of breath and sweating. Each time, his mother would rush to him, telling him that he had saved the children. "You're a hero, Daniel. Daddy and I are very proud of you." Daniel's father now understood the strength and courage that lay beneath the simple surface of his son. From that day on, his pride in his boy knew no bounds.

Indeed, everyone in Farrellville thought of Daniel as a hero and treated him with respect and affection. Sarah, although older than Daniel, became his best friend. Even Jimmy and Willy finally accepted him in the gang.

I was eight years old, the same as Daniel, when Granddad told me the story of the little boy who, by appearances, was not quite normal, but who showed that he was exceptional.

"Never judge people just by appearances but by who they really are. Get to know their character," said Granddad. It was the first time I had heard the expression "Never judge a book by its cover."

michael & *rebecca*

Do not let your hearts be troubled.
Trust in God; trust also in me.

John 14:1 (NIV)

Michael awoke to the alarm. *Awoke* is not the correct description, since Michael rarely slept soundly for more than an hour at a time. The red numbers on the clock showed five forty-five a.m. As he looked through the bedroom window, the sun was rising over the hills above Farrellville.

"Another day in this dead-end town," he mumbled to himself as he stumbled toward the bathroom. "This town is so far off of the beaten path you have to be lost to find it." He hated everything about his life in Farrellville, except for his family. But it wasn't always so with Michael.

He had spent his entire life here, and as a boy loved the small-town pleasures of fishing on the river, knowing everyone in town, playing ball with his friends at the schoolyard, and climbing those hills now becoming illuminated by the morning sun. He had never felt confined or limited but had seen his life in this town with unlimited possibilities. Although "average" in school, in sports, and, to be honest, in every other endeavor, he had nevertheless looked forward to each day as a new adventure.

In truth, he felt the only things in his life that were exceptional were his wife and daughter. He never understood how he had been so lucky to have Rebecca love him and marry him at such a young age. He attributed it to being in the right place at the right time. Living and growing up next door to Rebecca seemed utterly natural. He never gave a second thought to the happy circumstance of being with her virtually every day of his childhood. Childhood playmates became best friends. Finally, and unbelievably, the friends became high school sweethearts. To the consternation of both their parents, Michael and Rebecca decided to marry a year after graduating from high school. The plans and aspirations of their parents seemed to pale in comparison to living the rest of their lives together as husband and wife. Even Father Harley was enlisted to talk them out of it, but to no avail. At the ripe age of nineteen, Michael and Rebecca were married on a dreary, rainy Saturday in November at Our Lady of Perpetual Help Chapel. Neither noticed the weather, for to them the day was filled with sunshine.

Fourteen months later, Sarah was born. The pregnancy and delivery were particularly difficult for Rebecca, and only God's grace and the skill of Dr. Gordon allowed Sarah to be born healthy. Rebecca was not so lucky, and after complications and subsequent surgery, Dr. Gordon informed them that Rebecca could have no more children. It was at first a shock and great disappointment, but eventually, Michael and Rebecca considered themselves to be blessed, especially Michael, as Sarah grew into the image and likeness of her mother.

Life could not have been better for Michael. His love for cars as a teenager and his constant hanging around old man Hanson's garage resulted in a part-time job as an apprentice mechanic when he was a junior in high school. At the time of his marriage, he had risen to mechanic, and by the time Sarah was five years old, Michael was chief mechanic, essentially running the repair business. Two years later, the old man decided to hang it up and made Michael manager with the option to buy the business in five years.

Rebecca had gotten a secretarial position at the high school upon graduation, which led to an administrative assistant's job at the school board offices after Sarah's birth. While they weren't getting rich, they managed to get by with only occasional money problems.

Finally, an opportunity opened with the school district that would reduce her hours and still allow Michael and Rebecca to put away enough money to buy the garage. Rebecca would then be able to stay home full time, something Michael had always wanted for her.

To get the new position, Rebecca first had to get the proper license. After weeks of study, the day came for the

exam. She passed with flying colors and raced home to tell
Michael. To celebrate, they went into town for the most
expensive dinner at the Farrellville Inn.

So it was on the fateful day that defined Daniel's life,
Rebecca was driving the school bus as the 7:40 train
derailed. Only her quick reaction prevented a collision with
the engine, but the impact with the tree drove the steering
wheel into her chest. As the bus careened down the slope
toward the tree, her last thought was a prayer, *Mother Mary,
save Sarah!*

Michael arrived at the hospital just as the surgeon
exited from the operating room. "Doctor, how's Rebecca?
They told me she was badly hurt. Is she going to be all
right?"

"I'm sorry, Michael. There was nothing we could do."

Michael's mind went blank. He couldn't comprehend
what the doctor had just said. "But, but she …" he stammered.

"Sit down over here, Michael," said the doctor as he led
Michael to a chair.

"She can't be. I want to see her. Rebecca, Rebecca!" he
yelled.

"Michael, please, sit down for a minute. I need to tell
you about Sarah."

"Sarah? I thought she got out of the bus."

"She did, but has some severe cuts on her arms. Fortunately, no arteries were cut, but she required extensive
stitches to close them."

"Will she be okay?" Michael asked.

"Yes, but I'm afraid that there will be scarring," the doctor said.

Michael bent over with his head in his hands, "How...why did this happen?"

"From what I was told, Rebecca saved all of the children on the school bus by her quick reaction in avoiding the train. And Sarah was pulled out of the bus by young Daniel. I can't answer you, Michael, as to why it happened. I can only tell you that because of Rebecca and Daniel more lives were spared." ˙

"I want to see Sarah! Where is she?"

"Come with me. They should be finished with her arms by now."

Seeing Sarah in that bed with her arms wrapped from shoulder to wrist, still under the anesthetic, appearing to merely sleep, raised conflicting emotions in Michael. He was glad that she appeared to be without pain but angry that she had been injured. It was so unfair!

The next few days were a blur to Michael, except for the look on Sarah's face when he told her about Rebecca. Holding her as tears streamed down his face, he could not find the words to console her. How could he give her a reason that her mother was gone when he couldn't understand it himself.

The funeral mass and burial had been the hardest thing Michael had ever endured.

He had to show strength for Sarah's benefit, while all the day feeling as if he were falling into a black pit.

Falling into a black pit is how he had felt every day of the past six months, and as he prepared for work that morning Sarah was already up fixing breakfast for them. She was adjusting to Rebecca's absence better than he was, probably because her faith, instilled by Rebecca, was stronger than his. However, the scars on her arms were an embarrassment for her, and she now wore only long sleeves to hide them from view. As he finished dressing and tying his shoes, the dark hole deep inside of him started to swallow him for another day. "God, why did you do this to us? Why did you do this to her? Mother Mary, Rebecca was devoted to you. Why didn't you save her?"

As he said that, Michael felt a presence in the bed-room. A small glow extended from the ceiling. Suddenly, he heard—no, sensed—a woman's voice.

"Michael, why do you despair so?" The voice seemed familiar. *Was it Rebecca? No, it couldn't be. She is gone forever,* he thought.

"Michael, death isn't forever. That's not God's plan for us."

"Rebecca! Is that you?"

"Michael, Mother Mary answered my prayer in the school bus. She sent Daniel to save Sarah."

"But why did God do this to you?"

"He gave me a gift. I am with him now and forever, as we all shall be one day. You must have faith, Michael, to trust in him. Sarah understands this. Learn from her. Help her to overcome her embarrassment about her arms. Her beauty is not her appearance but her soul."

"I don't think I can," Michael said as the glow began to fade.

"Trust, Michael. Have faith in him."

"Don't leave me!"

"I'll always be here with you and Sarah."

As Michael sat on the bed, the darkness seemed to recede, and he felt a sense of hope, not despair. His lifelong faith, he thought lost in the dark hole, was still there. But somehow, he sensed, it was different. It had been given new life. Maybe, if he could just give it a chance it could grow. He would try.

Granddad introduced me to Michael when I was eleven, when I began to question my faith and expressed bitterness toward God about taking my mother at an age when I could not remember her. He told me that Michael had overcome his bitterness by his faith that God wanted good for us. "For us, death is the great mystery which seems to contradict that belief," Granddad said. "Do you remember when Father said at Mass on Sunday, that 'Life is a gift from God'?"

"Sure, Granddad," I answered.

"Well, I think it's like a birthday gift," he said. "This life is the box, the shiny wrapping paper, and the colorful ribbon. But to get the real gift inside, you must cut the ribbon, tear away the paper, and open the box. I think that's what death is—the removal of this life to get the real gift, eternal life with God in his kingdom, with all of our family and friends who have gone before us." That day, Granddad taught me that instead of looking backward, wondering what I had missed, I should look forward to meeting my mother when my gift is opened.

sarah

It is in giving of ourselves that we receive.

Prayer of St. Francis

Sarah remembered the morning that things changed for her dad. She had been fixing breakfast when he came out of his bedroom. Somehow he looked different, not as tired and bitter as previous mornings.

"Hi, Dad. I'm fixing eggs and bacon. Want some?"

"In a minute, honey," he replied. "Sarah, I know it's been hard since your mother ... I haven't done a very good job of helping you through it. It's been tough for me ..."

"I know, Dad."

"But you seem to be dealing with it better than me, honey."

Well, I ... you see ... I mean, Mom helped me."

"Helped you?'

"Yeah. When I was in the hospital."

"When did you see Mom then? I thought she was unconscious the whole time."

"I dunno, Dad. I think I was asleep when she came into my room. I didn't exactly see her, but I heard her voice."

"She-she spoke to you?" he asked.

"I guess so. I just heard her."

"What did she say to you?"

"She said that she had to go away for a while, that she would be okay, and that I shouldn't be sad. She told me to take care of you, Dad."

"Of me?"

"Yeah. She said that your faith wasn't strong enough yet. That you needed my help to make it stronger."

"My faith?"

"That's what she said."

"I-I guess she was right. I just thought I'd lost her forever."

"Not forever, Dad! We'll see her in heaven."

"I just wasn't sure of that, honey—until this morning. I heard Mom's voice in the bedroom!"

"You did?"

"She told me we'd be together again. That I should have you help me."

"I will, Dad."

"I know, honey. You've been trying all the time. I just wasn't accepting it. I will now," Michael said.

"I'm glad, Dad."

Sarah hugged her dad while the bacon burned and the eggs scorched. Sarah smelled the smoke. "Oh, the bacon is burning!"

As she shut off the burners, Michael said, "Don't worry, breakfast is on me this morning. We'll stop at the diner on the way to school."

So began Michael's journey without Rebecca; one which still left a large void in his heart, but now had hope and faith as well.

For Sarah, another journey began. Her sensitivity to the scars on her arms was reflected in the long sleeves that she insisted on wearing. Other kids were bad enough with their constant questions. "How are your arms?" "Do they still hurt?" "Are the scars going to go away?" But the adults were worse with their concern and pity. She knew that they meant well, but was tired of their attempts to cheer her up. Dad hadn't been helpful, because he was trying to deal with his loneliness. It was as if he ignored her wounds, then his pain may be ignored too.

But at the diner that morning, he started to ask her about how she felt about the scars. Other than making sure that the bandages were changed and the visits to the doctor were made, he hadn't seemed to care before.

"The pain is gone finally, isn't it?" he asked.

"Yes," she answered.

"But the hurt of the scars hasn't?"

"No, Dad."

"You're self-conscious about them. Is that why you cover them?"

"I don't like people staring or asking questions, that's all!"

"Well, I guess I can understand that. It's like everyone tries to be nice about Mom, but they don't feel what we lost."

"I guess."

"Sarah, the doctors did a pretty good job of fixing the cuts, but your arms were badly damaged. I don't think the scars will completely go away. But in time, they won't be as visible as they are now."

"They're so red and swollen, Dad."

"Yes, but in time that will go away."

"But they'll still show, won't they?"

"That's what the doctor said, honey."

"Sometimes, I wish Daniel hadn't pulled me through that window."

"Don't blame him, Sarah. He saved your life."

"I know, but…"

"Have you talked to Daniel about that day?"

"Not really. I tried to thank him, but he didn't want to talk about it. He said that he was still having bad dreams about the bus."

"Has he said anything about your arms?"

"He just said that he was sorry that he hurt me."

"You know, I think Daniel needs our help. What do you think, honey?"

"I don't know."

"Let's both think about it."

Over the next few weeks, Sarah thought about it a lot. How could she help Daniel? She also thought about how she could help her dad with his faith.

A funny thing happened in that time. As she spent more time thinking about helping both of them, she thought less about herself and her arms. Her dad seemed to be paying more attention at Mass on Sundays, and he was even praying with her at bedtime, which turned out to be one of her favorite times of the day. Together, they didn't say just the normal prayers to Jesus and Mary, but afterward they would sit and talk to Mom, as if she were there in the bedroom. Sarah and Dad would tell Mom about their day, the good things and the bad, the funny and the sad.

At first, Sarah told Mom her feelings about her arms, and Dad would talk about how lonely he felt. But eventually, they spent less time talking about themselves and more time asking how they could help Daniel.

One night Sarah decided to become Daniel's best friend. She would stop being shy about her arms because she knew that Daniel's concern would be real. He wouldn't ask her stupid question like other kids.

In the days and weeks that followed, Sarah did become Daniel's best friend. He never asked her silly questions about her scars, and he never pitied her. They learned to talk to each other about that day on the riverbank. She listened quietly as he relived that dreadful day. They both came to realize and communicate the unique bond that experience had forged between them. He stopped having the bad dreams, and she became less conscious of her scars.

Sarah became a friend of mine when I was twelve years old, when all I thought about was me: my wants and desires, my worries and cares, my likes and dislikes. I gave little attention or care to others. My Granddad saw this and decided that I needed a friend like Sarah, someone who had suffered great loss and who, at one time, saw only her scars. He knew that the lesson that Sarah had learned would be valuable to me. So he taught me: "It is by helping others that we most help ourselves."

anna

*Love is patient, love is kind. It does not envy,
it does not boast, it is not proud. It is not rude,
it is not self-seeking, it is not easily angered,
it keeps not record of wrongs. Love does not delight
in evil but rejoices with the truth. It always protects,
always trusts, always hopes, always perseveres.*

1 Corinthians 13:4–7 (NIV)

The old lady sat on the porch of the white house on the tree-lined street. Located a block from Main Street, she could see the clock tower on the Village Green. The tower bell had just chimed the three rings for midafternoon.

Granddad pointed to her, "See that lady on the porch, Sean?"

"Yes," I answered.

"Her story is about love and trust," Granddad said. "You must hear it."

"Why?" I asked.

"I want you know how they are similar and how they differ. Some people only learn it the hard way. By then it's too late."

"Okay," I said.

"The lady's name is Anna."

Anna had two sons, Robert and Harlan. Her husband died when the boys were young, and she was left to raise the boys alone. Anna was devoted to her boys and loved them for who they were. She tried never to compare them, for each had their own aptitudes and interests. There were times, however, when she wished they would engage in more activities together. She hoped that the boys would support each other in their pursuits, even if they didn't completely understand their brother's interests. Without her husband, Anna tried to fill the role of both parents. In her honest moments, she could see that she probably tended to spoil the boys. There were times when they needed the tough love that a father could bring. Both boys became self-absorbed with their own interests and activities. Each was also jealous of her attention, measuring and comparing her love for each of them.

Robert, the older son, was a gentle boy who loved to read. With his great imagination, he would create imaginary friends and adventures and eventually turned to writing. Anna loved to read his stories and discuss the characters with him. But Robert became a loner, preferring his own company to that of others.

Harlan, on the other hand, was more physical and energetic. He was constantly outdoors playing some game. It seemed to Anna that he was always on the move.

As they grew, their talents manifested themselves in school while their personalities and character solidified. Robert, the student, excelled in school and was consistently at the top of his class. Unfortunately, he came to see other people as inferiors and not worth his time. Harlan, the athlete, played all sports and was considered a star. He loved the spotlight that his athletic prowess brought him, becoming egotistical, always seeking attention from others. Thus, their relationships with those around them were affected. Robert became more withdrawn and isolated, while Harlan's friendships were superficial and lasted only as long as others continued to praise him, boosting his ego.

Since each were jealous of their mother's love for the other, the animosity grew between the brothers. When it came time for Robert to select a college, he had scholarship offers from many prestigious schools. He selected the one farthest from Farrellville. He wanted to be away, especially, from his brother, but also from his mother, who he believed favored Harlan over him. He returned home only for the Christmas holidays. During the summers, he took extra classes, which facilitated his graduation in three and a half years. Robert then went on to graduate school, earning advanced degrees. He became a professor at a prestigious university on the East Coast and remained withdrawn and secluded in his relationships with others. He returned to Farrellville occasionally to visit his mother but remained alienated from Harlan.

For his part, Harlan's promising athletic career was

derailed by a knee injury during a football game in his senior year of high school. The resulting surgery allowed him to walk normally but not to compete in collegiate sports. No longer the "golden boy" of the athletic fields, he became bitter and withdrawn. With the promise of an athletic scholarship to a university gone, Harlan lost interest in school and dropped out in his final semester of high school. Nothing Anna said would get him to change his mind. She realized that Harlan's self-image was based on the prestige that his athletic prowess brought him. Harlan moved from one part-time job to another, with no apparent purpose or direction.

One day in early spring, Harlan told Anna that he was leaving Farrellville.

"Where will you go?" she asked.

"I don't know, but I've got to get out of this town."

"But all of your friends are here, Harlan."

"Maybe they were when I was the big star, but now nobody pays attention to me."

"You're looking for the wrong attention," Anna said. "You don't give them a chance to get close to you now. You've withdrawn and shut people out. Sure, some of your former friends only wanted to be around the star and share in that popularity, but others liked you for who you really were. How about Sarah and Daniel? You have turned your back on them, Harlan."

"Sarah is a nice person, but she just pities me. And Daniel, well, he's just slow and would be friendly to anyone who would talk to him."

"You're the one pitying yourself, Harlan. Don't be so self-absorbed. Sarah and Daniel are true friends, and you are too stubborn to see it. Getting out of Farrellville isn't the solution. You need to get out of your own self-absorption. And you could start with your own brother!"

"You would bring him up, wouldn't you? You've always taken his side!"

"That's not true, Harlan. I don't know why there is this jealousy between you boys, but I love you both. Each of you seems to ignore that."

"I don't want to talk about it," Harlan said. "I just want to get a fresh start somewhere else."

"Will you at least stay until next Monday so we can have Easter dinner together?"

"Sure, Mom. I'll spend Easter with you."

"Thank you, Harlan. I'll fix your favorite dinner," Anna said.

⁂

Days later, Anna sat on her porch, feeling heartbroken that both of her boys, one highly successful in his field and the other moving aimlessly, had isolated themselves from each other and the people around them. With Robert's occasional calls and infrequent short visits home, and now with Harlan leaving, Anna feared that she had lost her boys. She had just returned home from Good Friday services, where she had asked God for help and guidance. Surely he would understand, since he lost his son on that Friday so many years ago.

As the sun descended behind the hills and the purple

. E. Brock

twilight fell over Farrellville, Anna rose from her rocking chair and started for the front door. She caught the heel of her shoe on the rocker and fell against the porch rail, striking her head. As she slipped into unconsciousness, she tried to call for Harlan but could not speak. Lying on the porch, darkness overtook took her as the nighttime engulfed Farrellville.

Having finished working on his car, Harlan walked from the garage to the house to wash up. "Mom? When will dinner be ready? Do I have time to shower?" he called out to the empty kitchen. *She must be on the porch,* he thought.

"Mom!" he cried when he saw Anna crumpled against the rail. He picked her up and took her into the living room. Turning on the light, he exclaimed, "Oh, God!" as he saw the bloody wound on her head.

It took but ten minutes for the emergency medical team to respond to his 911 call. Anna was still unconscious, and had weak readings as they tested her vital signs. Harlan held her hand as the ambulance rushed to the hospital, but could get no response from her.

≈≈≈

Hours later, Harlan paced the waiting room while Anna underwent surgery. He had talked to Robert as they took Anna into surgery, and said that he would call back when Doctor Avery came out to report her condition. Robert had called an hour ago, impatiently demanding an update.

"I can't give you any news, Robert. She is still in the operating room."

"Can't you get someone to go in and find out what is happening?" Robert demanded.

"Robert, back off! Everyone that knows anything is in the operating room trying to help her. I said that I would call you as soon as I get any news."

"Fine, but call me on my cell phone. I'm leaving now to drive there."

"Okay, come straight to the hospital.

"I'll see you in five hours," Robert said.

"I'll call you when I hear something," Harlan said as he heard the line disconnect.

Another hour went by before the doctor emerged from the double doors that separated the operating suite from the waiting room. "Harlan," Doctor Avery said as he took Harlan's arm and directed him to the chairs in the corner, "your mother has had a serious head injury."

"How serious?" Harlan asked.

"She has a skull fracture, and there is bleeding in the brain. We've tried to relieve the pressure from the swelling. We think we've been successful, but the next few hours will be critical. Her vital signs have improved, somewhat, but are still weak."

"Is she conscious yet?"

"No, she is still under the anesthetic."

"Is she going to live?"

"It's touch and go. We've done everything we can for right now. We have to see whether the swelling diminishes."

"Was there permanent brain damage, doctor?"

"Harlan, it's too early to tell. We're going to have to take this one step at a time."

"I know, Doctor. It's just that I have to call my brother, and he is going to have all of these questions."

"Unfortunately, the answers will take some time," Doctor Avery said. "We'll inform you as soon as the situation changes, Harlan."

"Thank you, Doctor."

As Harlan expected, Robert barraged him with questions when he called him. Finally, Harlan cut him off, "Look, Robert, I've told you all I know. When you get here, you can ask all of the questions you want. It doesn't appear that we'll know anything more before then. Unless … well …"

"Yeah, I know, Harlan," interjected Robert.

"Get here as quick as you can, Robert."

"I'm coming."

"Be careful, will you?"

"Yeah. Hang in there, Harlan," Robert said as he hung up.

Five hours and fifteen minutes after leaving, Robert walked into the hospital waiting room. He reported to the nurse at the window, who directed him to the intensive care recovery room where Harlan sat beside their mother's bed. It was a scene Robert would have etched in his memory forever. Harlan looked as if he had aged ten years and hadn't slept in a week. But the visage of his mother was the most unsettling. She looked small and frail, framed by the white linens of the hospital bed, but somehow peaceful. She wasn't the image of the robust, resourceful woman that he carried in his mind. *How has she aged so? Where is that stern, remote mother who doted on my little brother? Is this the mother who alienated me by directing her love to Harlan? Could it be that I created this image because of my own selfishness and jealousy?* All of these questions filled his mind.

Somehow, for the first time in many years, Robert saw his mother as she really was. He suddenly remembered the times she told him of her love for him, which he had dismissed out of a twisted view of their relationship. He remembered the years that she worked two jobs to support her boys, the long hours, and the weariness she displayed at the end of the day. A wave of emotion swept over him as he stood in the doorway. *How could I have been so selfish and self-centered not to see what was always before me?* he thought.

Harlan was so focused on Anna that he didn't hear Robert enter. Only when Robert touched his shoulder did he recognize that his brother had arrived.

"Robert!" Harlan said softly as he rose from the chair.

"Harlan. How is she?"

"No change since I talked to you. She hasn't awakened, and as you can see, her vital signs are unstable and weak.

"Why does she look so peaceful?" Robert asked.

"She's been like that since I came in," Harlan said.

"Can I talk to the doctor?"

"He said that he would be back to check on her at six o'clock … in about ten minutes," Harlan said as he checked the clock on the wall.

Robert pulled a chair from the waiting room to sit next to Harlan. He wanted to ask a hundred more questions of Harlan but realized that he didn't have the answers. In ten minutes, hopefully the doctor would have good news to give them. So the two brothers now sat together watching the one person who tied their lives together.

When Doctor Avery arrived, he reported that not much had changed. They had stopped the bleeding in brain, but the swelling was still the primary danger. Anna's vital signs had not deteriorated, but they were still unstable. He assured the brothers that all that could be done was being done. "We will have to wait and watch. In cases like this," he added, "and knowing the faith that your mother has, prayer may be the best thing we can do."

"Well, Doctor, neither of us have the faith that she has, and we're not big in the prayer department," Harlan replied.

"I see," Doctor Avery said. "Well, that's a personal thing. But there is a saying that even though you don't believe in God, he believes in you."

"Is that what you really think, or are you trying to give us false hope?" Robert asked.

"At this point, I think we could use all the help we can get. I'll be back at noon, unless things change. Will you boys be staying here?"

"Yes, Doctor," Robert said.

Doctor Avery returned at noon, but not much had changed. Anna had not regained consciousness. The brothers remained at her bedside, with only breaks to eat in the cafeteria in the hospital basement. The hours by her bedside did give them the opportunity to consider how their lives had diverged. They finally started talking to each other, seemingly for the first time in their lives, without being defensive and self-absorbed.

They began to realize that each carried similar destructive attitudes toward their brother, which also spilled over into their relationships with other people. They started to understand that the attitudes were within them and not with others. They remembered how their mother would try to get them to realize their self-destructiveness. Suddenly they could recall her voice communicating her love for them together and as individuals—the voice that each of them had stopped hearing.

❧

As evening turned into night, and night into early morning, two brothers, so long estranged, began to feel the love that their mother had always held for them, which neither of them trusted. Yet, in spite of their distrust, that love endured and remained unconditional. They remembered her lessons about love.

"Love is not manmade. We humans aren't capable of creating such a thing. Love is that part of us that is a gift of God himself. God's creation of us out of nothing is so wonderful that we should be on our knees every day, thanking him. But he didn't stop there. He gave us a soul, a part of him—love. It gave us the ability to know his love for us. It also gave us the gift of loving one another and to see God in each of us." They could hear her say, "People think love is soft, fuzzy, fragile, and can be destroyed. Nothing is further from the truth. Love is tough, durable, and eternal. It is trust that is fragile. It has to be given freely but can be withdrawn quickly and withheld forever."

Recalling her words during this long, dark night, they realized that their trust had been broken by their own selfishness. They had placed barriers to her love. They also realized now that their love for each other lay under the weight of distrust. Accepting their mother's love allowed them to find their love for each other and, more importantly, for themselves.

As the first light of that Easter Sunday morning filtered through the window, it shined on two brothers praying together at the bedside of a small, frail woman with a peaceful countenance. Both were startled by a hand gently touching each of their shoulders. As they looked into the eyes that had been closed these long hours, they heard her voice say softly, "My boys."

⊱⊰

"Did she recover fully, Granddad?" I asked as he concluded the story of Anna.

"Not entirely," he answered. "In spite of months of therapy, she was confined to a wheelchair. She was not able to work."

"What did she do?" I asked.

"It's not what she did, but what her sons did that is important. Harlan did not leave Farrellville. He stayed and went to trade school and graduated at the top of his class. His tuition was paid by Robert, who took over support of their mother until Harlan got his position in computer technology in the next town. Harlan continued to live in Anna's house and took care of her daily needs with the assistance of a day nurse they hired. Harlan learned to trust his friendship with Daniel and Sarah, and eventually he opened himself to love. Recently, Harlan and Sarah were married. Robert was the best man, and Daniel, as a groomsman, wore a tux for the first time in his life."

Granddad went on to explain that Robert continued in the academic life but moved to a university that was less prestigious, only an hour from Farrellville. He was a fixture every Sunday for dinner with Anna and Harlan, and, eventually, Sarah.

"Now, as you can see," Granddad said, "Anna sits on her porch with a peaceful smile."

If you listen closely, you can hear her say, "My boys!"

jack & *connor*

If you wish success in life, make perseverance your bosom friend, experience your wise counselor, caution your elder brother, and hope your guardian genius.

Joseph Addison

Jack ran past the gas station and turned the corner onto Main Street. He could see the finish line ahead. Connor ran a step behind his left shoulder. Sweat streaming into his eyes, blurring his vision, Jack tried to focus solely on the finish line and not on the fatigue he was feeling. His legs were aching, and his lungs burned, but he was determined to keep up the pace he had established this whole race.

It was the annual Farrellville 10k Race. Jack had been training for it all year. At first, he couldn't complete half of the distance, but over time, he built his stamina to cover the entire course. Today, the goal was to establish his best time ever, a new record for him!

"Keep focused. Keep up the pace," he said to himself. He looked over his shoulder at Connor. He was still there keeping pace with him. Connor was the best athlete in the school, whom Jack had looked up to all of these years and whom Jack wanted to be like—to be a winner! He wanted to win awards and trophies as well. However, as hard as he tried, Jack realized that there would be none with his name on it. He wasn't jealous of Connor; he just once wanted to experience the thrill of victory.

For Connor, it seemed all too easy. He was tall for his age and gifted with coordination and physical abilities that made any athletic endeavor as natural as breathing. He could run, throw, kick, and leap with a motion that was fluid and graceful. The closest comparison that Jack could think of was a dancer. Connor seemed to do these things as if to a melody that only he could hear.

Jack saw himself as awkward, uncoordinated, and definitely non-athletic. But that didn't stop him from trying anyway. He knew most sports were beyond him, but running he could do. He set as his goal the 10k race. He had seen Connor cross the finish line as the winner in his age group for the last three years.

The race started and finished on Main Street in front of the clock tower on the Village Green. The Green was filled with people who would picnic and party after the race. The streets would be lined as well with folks from the town and surrounding farms who had come into town to celebrate the Fourth of July. The morning would be focused on the race, while the afternoon was for picnics, games, and, of course, boring speeches from the mayor and local politicians, followed by the awarding of the 10k ribbons for the various age groups. The final award was the Outstanding Runner Trophy, given to the contestant with the best achievement of the day. In the evening, there was patriotic music and the grand fireworks finale.

Jack pressed on. The finish line was only a block away. He pushed himself harder. *Keep up the pace. Keep up the pace,* he thought over and over. He could see his parents beyond the finish line, cheering him on. He looked quickly over his shoulder again. Connor was still there, stride for stride. With twenty-five yards to go, he caught his left toe on the pavement and almost stumbled. He regained his balance just in time and stepped up his pace. *That was close,* he thought. *Now for the big finish!*

At the finish line, he leaned forward and immediately checked his stopwatch on his wrist. He'd done it! He had beaten his best time by fifty seconds! As he bent over, trying to catch his breath, he felt Connor's arm around his shoulder. "Great race, Jack. Congratulations!" he said.

That evening, Jack stood with his parents in front of the large gazebo, where the mayor was presenting the first-place ribbons to the top finishers in each age group. Jack was still in a sort of daze, thinking about the time he had achieved that morning. All day people had approached him with congratulations for his race.

Jack wasn't really listening to the mayor until he heard him say his name. Suddenly his mom and dad were patting him on the back and pushing him toward the steps of the gazebo. He looked up at his mom, who had tears in her eyes. "Go on up, Jack. You've been named the Outstanding Runner of the race!" she said excitedly.

Jack couldn't believe it. As he climbed each step, the trophy on the platform above seemed to get bigger and bigger. Reaching the platform, he realized that the trophy was over two feet tall with a golden figure of a runner on the top. It was the most beautiful thing he had ever seen!

"Congratulations, Jack. Great work!" said the mayor as he shook Jack's hand. Jack looked again at Mom and Dad and then at the crowd in the Green. All were cheering and applauding him.

Jack turned to Connor, who stood behind him with his first-place ribbon around his neck, and said, "Connor, I couldn't have done this without you."

Connor replied, "Sure you could, Jack. I just helped you do it a little faster."

"Can you help me lift it?" Jack said. "It's pretty heavy."

The trophy was lifted by Jack with his right hand and Connor with his left as the crowd chanted, "Jack! Jack! Jack!"

At this point in Granddad's tale of Jack and Connor, I was confused. "I don't understand, Granddad," I said. "I thought Jack beat Connor in the race."

"Oh, no!" Jack could never beat Connor," Granddad said. "You see, Jack had a condition at birth that prevented the full development of his left leg and arm. His left arm never grew straight, and his hand had only stubs for fingers. His left leg was shorter that the right, and his foot was turned in so much that the doctors told his parents that it was unlikely that he would ever walk without crutches. But walk he did, although much later than other kids. And as you have heard, through determination and perseverance, he learned to run as well; albeit slowly and with a severe gait."

"But Granddad, you said that Connor was behind Jack at the finish," I replied.

"He was, but only after he had won the 10k with his best time as well. Connor ran as fast as he could, so as he crossed the finish line he could double back on the course and join Jack. He placed himself at Jack's left shoulder and set the pace as he had done during every training run that Jack made that year. He whispered in Jack's ear 'Keep up the pace.' Connor wore two watches on his wrist, one for his time and one for Jack's. Connor was Jack's brother and a year and a half older. As I told you, Jack admired his brother. But Connor also had great admiration for Jack. He saw the physical effort it took for Jack to do the most common things that Connor took for granted."

"Did Connor feel sorry for Jack?" I asked.

"No," Granddad said. "Jack wouldn't let him. Jack didn't want pity, just acceptance and respect. So when Jack told Connor after the race the previous year that he wanted to run it the following year, Connor didn't question it. He had seen that determined look in Jack's eyes before when he had overcome other obstacles. 'Okay,' Connor said. 'I'll help you train.' Over that year, the brothers trained together. Connor worked with Jack to establish a gait that he could maintain over a long distance. After initial difficulty, with great effort, Jack mastered it. Then it became a matter of building endurance."

Jack remembered the first day he covered the entire ten kilometers without stopping. Connor thought he had accomplished his goal, but Jack wasn't satisfied. He wanted now to set time targets. So the final two months they worked on increasing the pace and shortening the time. Once a pace was established in Jack's mind, Connor would move ahead to work on his times. As he finished his 10k, he would come back to Jack and trot with him to set the pace the he needed to reach his target. Jack's hard work set an example for Connor, who at times in the past let his natural ability carry him. So Connor learned a lesson from Jack about work ethic and became a better runner.

"Together, two brothers used teamwork to achieve success," Granddad explained. "Connor was a winner, and Jack was a victor."

Throughout my life, when I think of success, I remember Granddad's lesson of Jack and Connor. "Success is fulfillment of our potential. Potential is like a pot of gold that has to be used in this life, because you can't take any leftovers when you depart."

lauren & *rachael*

Don't walk behind me, I may not lead.
Don't walk in front of me, I may not follow.
Just walk beside me, and be my friend.

Unknown

One day, during a visit to Farrellville, the subject of friendship came up in our conversation. "Friendship, next to family, is one of the strongest bonds a person can have," Granddad said. "A good friend is a treasure that must be valued as such."

"I have lots of friends, Granddad," I replied.

"I'm sure that you do, Sean. But I'm not talking about casual friendships. The kind of friendship I'm referring to is so special that most of us are lucky to have one or two in our lifetime."

"I'm not sure what you mean, Granddad."

"Maybe this will help." And so, Granddad told me the story of two girls who grew up in Farrellville.

Lauren and Rachael were friends. No, they were more than that. They were close, lifelong friends. The friendship went back before either of them could remember, having played together as toddlers as their parents played cards every Friday night. Since Lauren had no sister, only younger brothers, and Rachael was an only child, by the time they entered elementary school, Lauren and Rachael were inseparable. As both girls were tall for their age and had similar-colored hair, strangers often thought they were sisters. Their interests led them to taking the same dance classes, joining the same Brownie troop (their mothers shared the troop mother duties), singing in the school chorus, and, of course, sharing a great dislike for Jimmy Swatmore, Willy Packard, and their stupid gang. They did like Daniel though, because he was so nice, not a smart aleck like Jimmy and Willy. After Daniel saved them and their classmates on that school bus, they had respect for him as well.

Intellectually they complimented one another; Lauren was adept at math and science, while Rachael excelled in English, history, and social sciences. Through middle and high school, they tutored each other, with the result that Rachael was in the top 15 percent of their graduating class, and Lauren was valedictorian. It was upon graduation that their paths diverged. Lauren had received a scholarship to a private college out of state. Rachael planned to commute to the state university thirty miles from Farrellville. While each was excited for the other, they were a bit worried that separation would be more difficult than they realized.

⁊⁊⁊

Rachael and Lauren never really talked about the separation until late one August evening while sitting in the backyard after Lauren's going away party.

"Sometimes I wish I hadn't accepted that scholarship so we could go to school together at state," Lauren said.

"Don't be silly, you worked hard for that. You earned it, and taking it was the right thing to do," Rachael replied. "Besides, you'll be coming home for the holidays, and we'll have summers together."

"I know but … well, who will I talk to about … you know, all of the things that we talk about."

"What? They don't have telephones at that expensive college?"

"Oh, you know what I mean. It's not the same as lying across the bed while you sit on the floor painting your toenails and talking about boys and clothes and school," Lauren said.

"Look, no matter how far apart we are, or for how long, we'll always be close. Right?"

"Absolutely! Nothing comes between us. Lauren and Rachael forever!"

⁊⁊⁊

But separation did eventually come, both in time and distance. Lauren did return that first year for the holidays and summer vacation, but in her second year, she received an internship that kept her from returning home. Her third year was spent studying abroad, but she did come home at Christmas. Even with the separation, the girls found that immediately upon being together they picked up as if Lauren had never been gone.

Rachael continued to commute to State for the first two years. By her third year, she had saved enough to get a small apartment near campus. A part-time job at the college bookstore provided enough income to supplement the small financial assistance that her parents were able to provide. In her senior year, she and Connor were engaged. Since he had graduated the year before and was now the PE teacher and JV football coach at Farrellville High School, they planned to be married upon her graduation. With her degree in library science, she was able to get a job as assistant librarian at the Farrellville Library.

With Lauren as her maid of honor, the girls fulfilled a lifelong dream. The few weeks that Lauren was home for the wedding were a return to those "growing-up days" of two little girls. Between frantic hours and days of wedding preparations, the two friends spent late-night hours reminiscing, discussing Connor (about how lucky Rachael was according to Lauren, and how lucky he was, according to Rachael), and men in general, Lauren's career aspirations in medicine, and so on and so on. The fact that these nocturnal sessions occurred over many bottles of wine explained the lack of clarity by both of them as to what, if anything, was discussed, much less decided upon. They did agree, however, that those were some of the best times that they had ever had together.

The wedding was everything that both wished for. Lauren was so happy for Rachael, who was a radiant bride. As Rachael and Connor drove away to their honeymoon, neither of the friends realized that another separation had begun.

❦❦❦

That summer, Lauren was selected to be part of a medical research team. She spent the next two years in third-world countries, assisting the medical team in researching childhood diseases. This experience confirmed her desire to become a doctor, and channeled her interest toward pediatrics. In her correspondence to Rachael, she spoke of how she loved to work with children and of the heartbreak she experienced in seeing them ravaged by the diseases that she struggled to understand and defeat.

Upon her return, she spent three weeks in Farrellville. She and Rachael fell back into their old comfort zone as if she had never been away. Of course, there were changes in Rachael's life, namely young Brad, who was now twelve months old and toddling around the house. Rachael was excited for Lauren when she told Rachael that she had been accepted to medical school and that she would pursue a career in pediatrics. However, since the medical school was across the country, another separation was in store for the friends.

❦❦❦

Rachael settled comfortably into the life of a mother, which was a good thing, because a year later, twins, Brian and Ryan, arrived. Quitting her job at the library, Rachael became a stay-at-home domestic management director and caregiver, otherwise known as housewife and mother. Connor's career was taking off. He had been selected to replace the retiring head football coach at Farrellville High, Vern Barber. Connor considered this an honor, since he had played for Coach Barber, who was his inspiration for pursuing a coaching career. Though he was young for the head coaching position, his career as quarterback at Farrellville High and the state university made him a popular choice in the town.

During the years at medical school and her hospital residency, Lauren maintained regular correspondence with Rachael, reinforced by occasional visits home. It was during one of those visits that Lauren rediscovered, or more accurately was pursued by, Jimmy Swatmore. He always seemed to be around when she was in town. She was surprised that smart-alecky Jimmy had turned out to be a charming and attractive young man. The fact that he had a successful insurance business in town didn't hurt his chances either. With each visit home, Lauren and Jimmy spent more time together, finding that their attraction grew. Jimmy confided to her that she had been the apple of his eye since elementary school but he never had the courage to pursue her in high school because of his fear of rejection. But he always kept up with her through her parents, who had become his clients.

Therefore, on the last night before flying to the West Coast for her last few months of residency, Lauren stood on Rachael's porch and knocked lightly on her door.

When Rachael answered the door, Lauren said, "I hope I'm not too late. Jimmy and I had dinner tonight, and I told him that I needed to see you before I went to the airport in the morning."

"Of course not! The boys are in bed, and Connor is still meeting with his assistant coaches at the school. Big game this weekend, you know," Rachael said. "What's up? I can't remember seeing you look so excited. You're glowing!"

"I wanted you to be the first to know, after Mom and Dad, of course. Jimmy asked me to marry him!"

"And you said?"

"I said yes!"

"That's so great! I'm so happy for you, Lauren."

"We're planning the wedding for next summer after I've finished my residency. I'm applying for an open spot in pediatrics at Farrellville Hospital."

"That'll be wonderful!" Rachael said.

"Yeah, I hope I get it. I've wanted to come home for a while now. Traveling and living elsewhere has made me appreciate Farrellville so much more," Lauren said. "When Jimmy and I started seeing each other, it made me even more determined to return home."

"I'm so excited," Rachael said. "So when do you start planning for the wedding?"

"Well, I was hoping you would help me."

"Of course I will! What do you want me to do?"

"For starters, I want you to be my maid of honor."

"You got it!" Rachael replied.

"The second thing is my last term of residency will leave me will little spare time to help Mom make all of the arrangements. You know me better than anybody. Would you help her make choices that she can send to me for final selections?"

"Of course, silly! Your mom and I will have a great time trying to second-guess you."

"Thanks, Rachael. I knew I could count on you. Oh, look at the time. I've got to get home and finish packing. I'll call you tomorrow when I get back to the West Coast."

"Okay. I'll check in with your mom tomorrow and get the ball rolling. I'll also stop in to see Jimmy and let him know what he is getting himself into."

"Oh, he knows already. Besides, I'm the one who should have second thoughts. Can you imagine the terror a young patient of mine will experience when his mother tells him that he is going in to see Doctor Swatmore? I may have to keep my last name just to have a career."

Laughing, both girls hugged each other and said good night.

Just as Lauren had anticipated, the final months of residency seemed to occupy all of her waking hours, not counting the many nights that she slept in the hospital. Had it not been for Rachael's help with her mom, the wedding would never have made it on schedule. Lauren knew the effort it took on Rachael's part, especially with her three boys. Fortunately, after football season, Connor's schedule eased up, allowing Rachael some free time to help with the wedding arrangements.

Finally, the big day came! Everything came off without a hitch, that is, if you ignore the fact that Jimmy left her wedding ring at the house. His father had to make a last-minute mad dash from the church to retrieve it, while the organist vamped for about ten minutes with the longest rendition of the wedding march that anyone in Farrellville had ever heard.

Lauren got the pediatric position at the hospital and, upon their return from the honeymoon, started her career as Doctor Swatmore (yes, in the end, she decided that her young patients would just have to tough it out and learn to overcome their fears). Life was good for the two friends, who were now neighbors. It got even better when both learned the same month that they were pregnant! Each hoped for a girl, especially, Rachael. This was her and Connor's final attempt at having a girl, because she was starting to experience some difficulty with her kidneys. Her doctor was concerned about another pregnancy, but her condition was not serious yet.

꧁꧂

Eight months and thirteen days later, Rachael got her wish when her daughter was born. It took her and Connor only a moment to decide that Lauren Mary would be her name. Two weeks later, Lauren had a girl as well. She and Jimmy named her Rachael Anne. Of course, each couple selected the other to be godparents to their babies. So the circle had been completed. Once again, there were two girls named Lauren and Rachael.

"So is that how their story ends, Granddad?" I asked.

"No, Sean. Their friendship was to undergo the biggest test of their lives," Granddad answered.

Within a year of her daughter's birth, Rachael's kidney condition worsened to the point that she was hospitalized. The doctor decided that a transplant would be needed within the next two years. Rachael was put on the applicant list for kidney donations, while she commenced dialysis treatments. Through it all, Lauren helped with her children, along with Rachael and Connor's parents, even through her second pregnancy, which resulted in the birth of a son, Timothy Joseph.

At the two-year mark, a suitable donor had not been found for Rachael. Finally, Lauren, after much prayer and discussion with Jimmy, went to the doctor to be tested as a possible donor. The tests were positive. When Lauren broached the subject, Rachael refused.

"I can't let you do that! Think of your family."

"Rachael, Jimmy and I have discussed this, and he is supportive. We're not planning on having more children. I'm perfectly healthy and can do fine with one kidney."

"Oh, Lauren, I can't tell you how much this means to me. But I can't let you do it. I'll keep praying that God will find a donor from that list."

"Rachael, God has answered your prayer. Why do you think I'm a compatible donor? It's been his plan all along. It's why we became such close friends and remained so through all of our separations."

Finally, Lauren prevailed upon Rachael, who consented to the transplant. As the two friends were rolled into the operating room, Rachael reached out to grasp Lauren's hand.

"I love you, Lauren. God bless you."

"He already has. He gave me you as a friend."

Years later, Rachael and Lauren sat on Rachael's porch, watching two young girls playing together in the front yard.

"Mom," called Rachael Anne, "can Lauren and I walk downtown to get an ice cream?"

"Sure," answered Lauren. "As a matter of fact, ice cream sounds pretty good to me. How about you, Rachael?"

"You bet!" Let's go!"

Rachael reached out and put her arm around Lauren's shoulder as they followed two young friends, who were skipping hand in hand down the sidewalk.

angelina & *angelica*

*For he will command his angels
concerning you to guard you in all your ways.*

Psalm 91:11 (NIV)

One Sunday, during an extended stay with my grandparents while my father was overseas, I asked Granddad about the subject of the priest's homily at mass that morning.

"Granddad, do you believe what Father said about the angels?"

"What about angels?" he replied.

"You know. How they're part of this world, even though they're spirits."

"Well, I've never actually seen one, but let me tell you about a little girl who did. Her name was Angelina."

Angelica looked down at Angelina in her hospital bed. The family was with her because she was going home today. Angelica looked at her peaceful countenance and thanked God for the opportunity to be part of Angelina's life.

They had entered this life together. Angelica had preceded Angelina by moments, so close and yet so different in appearance and character. Angelina was the physical one, energetic, enthusiastic, and impetuous, whereas Angelica was the spiritual one, reserved, thoughtful, and able to see the "big picture" and not just the moment at hand. That's not to say that Angelina didn't have a spiritual side as well. Angelica could still remember that day driving with Grandma in the car when Angelina asked, "Grandma, have you ever seen angels?"

"Well, no. I don't believe I have," Grandma answered. "Have you?"

"I think so, Grandma."

"Where did you see them, dear?"

"I think I saw one in the kitchen, and another in the family room. I've seen them mostly in my bedroom when I wake up in the morning."

"What do they look like?"

"I'm not sure. I only see them out of the corner of my eye, and when I turn to look at them, they're not there. Do you know that they wear different colors, Grandma?"

"I didn't know that. What kind of colors?"

"The one in the kitchen was red, and the one in the family room was blue. The one in the bedroom is bright yellow like sunshine."

"Is that the one you see in the morning?"

"Yeah. Not every morning, just sometimes. When I open my eyes, I see the bright yellow in the corner of my eye; but when I turn my head, they're gone. It's funny, but they don't scare me, not like a ghost or anything like that. But I wish they would stay so I could see them."

"Do you hear them?

"No, they don't make any noise. Sometimes I call out to them, but I don't hear anything."

"Do you know much about angels?"

"Not much. You're the first person I've told about them, Grandma," Angelina said.

"Well, when we get to my house, I have a book that is about angels. We'll take a look at it."

Grandma's book told about the cherubim and seraphim, and, of course, the guardian angels. It said that angels are spiritual creatures that God has given certain duties on earth. The word *angel* comes from the Greek word *angelos,* meaning "messenger." The guardian angels were given by God to each person to guard and direct them on earth. They also intercede for us with God, and we should ask for their prayers for us.

Grandma went on to tell about angels that had been seen by people as related in the Bible. The book of Daniel describes the angels Gabriel and Michael. The book of Tobit tells of angel Raphael. "Also," Grandma said, "the Gospels tell of an angel appearing to Zachary to tell him that he will have a son. That son was John the Baptist. You're heard of him, haven't you?"

"Yes, Grandma."

"Of course, we all know of the story of Gabriel appearing to Mary to announce that she'll be the mother of Jesus."

"Oh, I love that story, Grandma," Angelina said.

"Then you know at Bethlehem choirs of angels appeared to the shepherds to announce that Jesus had been born. So, you see, angels have been with us since the beginning and are always with us. Most of us aren't lucky enough to see them, however," Grandma said.

"Mom taught me the 'Angel of God' prayer, and I say it every night."

"That's good. Ask the angel to watch over you and keep you close to God."

Angelina did. Each night Angelica could hear her say her prayers, which always concluded with, "Angel of God, my guardian dear..."

Here in the hospital, Angelica could still see Angelina as a young child, bright blue eyes, a freckled face framed by blonde curls that fell as ringlets down her back, always on the move, ramming full speed through the house or yard, always on some mission that required completion immediately. She was a happy, free-spirited girl. At times, she could test your patience, but any frustration that it caused was dissolved by her loving manner and the goodness of her heart. Angelica loved being with her. She was devoted to her and very protective of her.

Angelica's protection became even more important when Angelina turned fifteen and learned that she had a rare disease that attacked her immune system. Angelina suddenly became susceptible to viruses and bacteria that would be repelled by normal immune systems. Within months, she was fighting one disease after another. If not confined to bed, she was in a wheelchair, unable to walk, run, or play as other children. This was a crushing blow to her parents and family. Angelica saw the sadness of her family, and tried to help Angelina know that God loved her. Angelina understood that message and maintained a positive and prayerful attitude. She was constantly consoling those around her and talked of God's love. Her prayers became even more sincere and meaningful. She would smile when others were crying. Even through the pain and suffering of the many treatments that she had to endure, she never exhibited despair.

Sometimes in those private moments when Angelina and Angelica were alone, Angelina would start to feel discouraged and tearfully ask God, "Why?" Angelica would embrace Angelina and give her strength. So, Angelica helped Angelina bear her personal cross and serve as a positive influence on those around her.

Angelica remembered all of this as Angelina lay in the hospital bed. But now it was time for Angelina to go home. Opening her eyes, Angelina smiled as she looked at Angelica and said, "I see you. You're so beautiful. You are like the sunshine."

"Hello, my dear Angelina. I'm Angelica.

"You've always been there, haven't you?"

"Yes, I've been at your side since the beginning."

"My family is so sad. Will you help them?"

"Their faith is strong. Their guardians will help them accept God's love and overcome their sadness."

"I'm ready."

Angelica held out her hand. "I'll take you home now."

ellie

*Train a child in the way he should go, and
when he is old he will not turn from it.*

Proverbs 22:6 (NIV)

"Sean, remember the lesson when I told you about Daniel?"

"Sure, Granddad," I answered. "Don't judge people by their appearance, but by who they are. Judge them by their character."

"Very good! You did remember. But I didn't tell you what character was. There are a lot of definitions that people have. Some are pretty complicated. The one I liked the best is pretty simple and straightforward—'Character is what you do when no one else is around,'" Granddad said. "Does that make sense to you?"

"I think so," I replied.

"Let me introduce you to Ellie. I think her story can

illustrate what I mean. She had many instances in her life, as we all do, to make choices and decisions that revealed her character. I'll only tell you of her first one."

Ellie lived with her parents and older sister, Jennifer, in a small house on the edge of town near the train yards. Her father had been badly injured in an auto accident when Ellie was two years old, which left him permanently disabled and unable to work. Her mother worked as a waitress at the Farrellville Diner in town. Money was tight, but Ellie never thought of herself as poor, even though the clothes she wore were Jennifer's hand-me-downs, which had originally been purchased at the church thrift shop.

Her first test of character came when she was seven years old. After school, she would go the diner to wait until her mother was finished, and she would walk home with her. Since her mother worked the breakfast and lunch shifts, she was able to be home in the evenings to fix dinner. Ellie would sit in one of the rear booths and do her homework.

She loved the activity of the diner, the people coming and going, the cook in the back preparing and calling out the orders when ready, and Mom and the other waitresses hustling about, serving the customers at the counter and the booths. It was a Friday, and she was looking forward to the weekend. As she approached the diner, she saw something on the sidewalk just outside the door. When she stood over it, Ellie realized that it was a money clip with several bills in it. She looked around to see if she could tell who had dropped it, but no one was near. She picked it up and saw four twenties and a ten-dollar bill—ninety dollars. Ellie had never held that much money in her life. Think what she could get with ninety dollars! She could give it to her mom to pay bills.

There was nothing wrong with keeping it. Finders, keepers, right? She knew, however, that her mom wouldn't let her keep it, if she told. Maybe she would keep it to herself. Hide the money in her room and only spend a little at a time so nobody would notice. Whoever had lost it was probably rich enough that they could afford to lose ninety dollars. *I'll bet they don't even come back to look for it,* she thought.

But then, she heard a tiny voice in the back of her mind speak to her, *You can't keep this money. It belongs to someone else. You need to turn it in. It's the right thing to do.*

I know, she thought. Mom had told her about having a conscience. But this was the first time that she understood what her mother meant.

Opening the door to the diner, she went straight to her mother, who was standing behind the counter waiting for an order.

"Mom, can I talk to you for a minute?"

"Sure, honey. Go sit in the back booth while I get this order"

Mom served the order and walked over to the booth. "What's up?" she asked.

"Mom, I found this money on the sidewalk outside. I wanted to keep it and give it to you tonight so you could buy some groceries or something, but I knew you wouldn't keep it. A little voice in my head said that I should try to find who lost it."

"You're right, Ellie. I wouldn't keep the money, no matter how badly we need it. But I'm very proud that you listened to the voice and made that decision on your own. It means that you have a good conscience."

Just then, the front door opened, and Daniel came in. Mom got up from the booth and walked over to Daniel.

"Hi, Daniel! Did you decide to have that piece of pie after all?"

"Oh! No, Marge. I-uh-I...did you find...uh...I lost some money. I thought, maybe I left it here on the counter."

"Is this money clip yours?'

"Yeah! That's it. Where did you find it?"

"I didn't, but Ellie did. It was lying on the sidewalk just outside the door. She just brought it in."

"It must have fallen out of my pocket when I opened the door." Daniel turned and walked over to the booth. "Hi, Ellie," he said as he sat down in the booth.

"Hi, Daniel," Ellie replied.

"Your mom said that you found my money on the sidewalk and returned it to her."

"Yeah. I didn't know it belonged to you though"

"I want to thank you for your honesty. That was all the money I had until next payday. I would have been up a creek without it."

"That's okay, Daniel."

"Well, I can see that your mom taught you well. I'd like to give you five dollars as a reward. Let me go break this ten-dollar bill."

While Ellie would have been thrilled to have even the

five dollars, the little voice spoke to her again, *Remember that your Mom taught you to be honest for its own sake, not for rewards.*

"No, that's okay, Daniel. I don't need any reward. But thanks for the offer anyway."

"Well, all right Ellie. But I tell you what. I really wanted a piece of pie for dessert, and I don't like eating alone if I don't have to. I'd really appreciate it if you would have a piece with me. It'll be my treat!"

Ellie paused for a moment to see if that little voice was going raise an objection, but hearing none, she gladly replied, "Sure, Daniel. Do they have cherry?"

"Cherry sounds good to me too," Daniel said. He turned toward the counter and called out, "Marge, do you have cherry pie today?"

"Sure do, Daniel," she replied.

"Great! We'll have two pieces over here, pronto!"

john

*You cannot teach a man anything; you can
only help him to find it within himself.*

Galileo

One day I was complaining to Granddad about school,
especially about my math teacher, who I thought was too
tough on us kids.

"What do you mean?" Granddad asked.

"He's always testing us, giving us lots of homework,
and he doesn't give us good grades," I said.

"Good grades, huh. I thought your grades were pretty
good last semester."

"They were in most of my classes, but he gave me a C.
And do you know what he said when I asked him why he
gave a C?"

"I can guess, but you tell me anyway," Granddad said with a slight smile.

"He said that he didn't give me anything—it was what I earned. He told me that he knew I could do better."

"I see. Do you think you did your best in his class?"

"Well, no. But the other teachers gave me better grades, and I didn't do my best in their classes, except for English—I like English."

"Sean, one day you'll appreciate that teacher. He's just trying to get you to give your best effort. You're a bright young fellow. You can do better than C work in math."

"Well, maybe…"

"Sean, do you know what a mentor is?"

"I don't think so," I said.

"A mentor is a wise advisor, a trusted counselor. It seems to me that your math teacher fits that description. I think he is trying to teach you more than just math. He's trying to help you learn something about yourself that you can use for the rest of your life. Let me give you an example of how a mentor can change a person's life. I want to tell you about a young man named John."

John picked at his guitar as the bus raced down the highway toward Farrellville. He had been working on this song for a couple of weeks, but somehow the melody wouldn't come to him. He was close but couldn't get it right, and this one had to be right. The lyrics had come easy. All he had to do was remember a young boy and a music teacher named Isaac Gold.

As an orphan, living with his maternal grandmother, John had always felt like an outsider. He never seemed to fit in. His grandmother tried, Lord knows, but he lacked confidence in himself. He was an average student, a less-than-average athlete, and socially awkward. He sought attention by acting out in class, which lead to multiple trips to the principal's office, with the resulting call to his grandmother. John was labeled a problem child, which seemed to be his best claim for a reputation because he surmised that being known for something was better than not being known at all.

His only real interest seemed to be in the beat-up guitar that he had found in his grandmother's attic. Alone in his room, when he was supposed to be studying, he plucked and strummed, trying to put together chords and melodies. He would listen to music on the radio and try to emulate the guitar players he heard. Since his grandmother was a big fan of country and western music, those melodies were the ones he tried to master. Over time, he had taught himself to play several tunes. Once he learned the basic melody, he would try to improvise to create his own version. Some he liked; most he didn't.

When he entered high school, he convinced his grandmother to select the music class as his elective for the freshman year. While she wanted him to take a more academic course, which might direct him toward college, his enthusiasm swayed her. Therefore, on that first day of high school, fifth period, he entered Mr. Gold's music class, and his life changed forever.

"Good morning, class! My name is Mr. Gold. This is an introductory class in music appreciation. You will be introduced, probably for the first time, to various types of music, reflecting different traditions and cultures. Believe it or not, music does not begin and end with the pop music of today. At the end of the semester, it is my hope that each of you will use this introduction to pursue the type of music that interests you. That is my hope. However, having done this for over thirty years, I realize that only a few will actually pursue a music career."

As John sat at his desk, these words seemed to stir something within him. He'd never given any thought that music might offer a career for him. The longer he thought about it, the more plausible it seemed. Suddenly, he became aware of someone calling his name, which brought him out of his reverie.

"John Tyler," Isaac said for the third time as he continued with roll call of the class.

"Uh, here," John said.

"Mr. Tyler, the proper response is 'present.' *Uh* is not an expression that has any place in this class."

"Sorry, sir. I was thinking of something and didn't hear you."

"I hope it was about this class, Mr. Tyler, because I'll not grade you on any extraneous thoughts that might occur to you during our time together," Isaac said.

"Well, yes, sir. It was. Do you think one of us could have a career in music?"

"As strange and farfetched as that seems now, I have had a few students do so."

As Isaac continued with the roll call, John wondered if he could be one of the few. After class, John approached Isaac and asked, "Mr. Gold, what does it take to be a musician?"

Isaac replied, "First, you must have talent. Second, you have to nurture that talent. Third, you must have feeling for the music, to play it as an artist and not as a craftsman. Finally, if you are to create music, you must have something to express."

"How do I find something to express?" John asked.

"Mr. Tyler, it is my experience that you don't find it, but it will come from within you. Most creative people can't explain it; they only experience it when they open themselves to it. Do you think you have talent, Mr. Tyler?"

"I don't know, Mr. Gold. I have an old guitar that I play around with. I'm pretty good with learning melodies when I hear them but not so good at creating them."

"Okay, Mr. Tyler. If you apply yourself to this course and show me that you can work hard, I'll see if we can move you to Introductory Guitar next semester."

"I will, Mr. Gold. You'll see," John said.

≈⁂≈

So began John's journey in music and a relationship that would surprise both student and teacher. Many of the students who had taken this course, assuming that it was an easy elective, quickly learned otherwise. Isaac was demanding but fair. Students' grades reflected what they had earned. Grade inflation was not in Isaac's vocabulary. This is not to say that his demeanor was dour or negative. Quite the opposite. Applying oneself with hard work was rewarded with enthusiastic compliments, and students earned credit on their grades.

John did apply himself. The harder he worked, the quicker it came to him. This work ethic spilled over into his other studies, so that as the first semester ended, he had earned the best grades of his life. Isaac accepted him into Introductory Guitar, and he flourished under his teacher's firm and supportive direction.

As the freshman year ended, Isaac recommended that John be tutored in not only guitar but voice as well. John had discovered that he liked singing and had a good voice. When told by John's grandmother that she couldn't pay for a tutor, Isaac offered to privately tutor John for a small fee that she could afford. Fortunately, Isaac lived within walking distance from the grandmother's house. For the entire summer, John spent three days a week under Isaac's tutelage.

Over the next three years, John and Isaac formed a bond closer than just student and teacher. Isaac became the father figure that John never had. He learned life lessons that would carry him into manhood. Isaac saw in John a talent that he had not seen in his former students. John also worked hard to develop this talent and began to show true creativity. John's voice developed a style that fit his music creations perfectly. While his style was not classical, it had discipline and range. The music that John started to develop had a country quality about it. His lyrics told stories that flowed from his experiences and emotions. He could also do classic ballads of the forties with a feeling that belied his age.

Isaac realized that John's talents were soon beyond his ability to develop. He pursued acquaintances in the music business. He even contacted an old classmate who was an agent in the country music business in Nashville. He had John prepare audition tapes, which he sent to agents and production companies. Most he never heard from; some returned a form letter, which he suspected had been issued without listening to the tape.

John performed in school events and as a senior, got some social engagements around the county to play. He continued to write and developed an extensive repertoire that he could perform. It was no surprise that he received the top music award at graduation ceremony. What was surprising was that he was selected as a commencement speaker to offer remarks for the senior class. True to his nature, he composed a song that captured the high school experience for him and his classmates. He received a standing ovation.

John had received a scholarship to a prestigious music school in the East, and was preparing to enter in the fall when Isaac received a response from the agent in Nashville. He had listened to John's tape and was impressed with his voice. When Isaac told him that the songs were John's compositions, he said that he would like to meet John. Within weeks, John had to make the hardest decision of his life. The agent wanted him to move to Nashville under his direction and begin his career. He told him that it wouldn't be easy. It would involve short gigs as backup guitarist in bars and nightclubs, occasionally getting a backup session in a recording studio. He only promised him hard work, long hours, and low pay. It would, however, give him exposure to people who could affect his career. Giving up the scholarship, a prize that his grandmother treasured, was difficult to contemplate. When asked for his counsel, Isaac responded, "This is a decision that only you can make, John. Make it for yourself, not for your grandmother or me. Just remember that you'll need total commitment to make it in the music business." Isaac did not tell John that he had been faced with a similar decision years ago. He chose the certainty of the academic life because he recognized that he didn't have that commitment.

Ten years had passed since John made his decision, but he could still hear Isaac's words in his mind. After six years of hard work, living as a pauper, sometimes questioning the strong belief in himself, and finally a few lucky breaks, he became an overnight success as J.T. Tyler, country music star. Sitting in his customized bus, which served as his home while on tour, John finally found the melody that had been evading him.

Tonight, he would see Isaac Gold for the first time in a year and a half. He had produced another platinum album and had just completed a year-long promotional tour. However, he and Isaac were never far apart, as John would call him once a week, like clockwork, to discuss the weeks' activities. John had used Isaac as his touchstone to reality, which was even more important, since his grandmother had died two years ago. Fortunately, she had lived long enough to see that rejecting the music scholarship had been the right decision after all.

He stayed with Isaac for the three days that he was home. They were glorious hours, and it was just the break he needed from his highly stressful life. The old man told him of the decision he had made those many years ago.

"I always wondered if I could have made it," said Isaac as they sat on his back porch, drinking Isaac's homemade wine. "But I'm happy with my life. I've had the opportunity to open the world of music to young people, and in a few precious instances, to see talent emerge and illuminate the world with music that we might otherwise have never known." Raising his glass, Isaac said, "A toast to the best of all of those talents—to J.T. Tyler, whom it is my privilege to know as John, my student and friend."

That night, they attended the event that had brought John home to Farrellville. It was being held in the high school auditorium, where he had sung at commencement. Mr. Isaac Gold, director of the music department, director of the school band, and instructor for Introduction to Music Appreciation, was retiring. It had been John's idea, when notified that Isaac had reached mandatory retirement age, that he put on a concert to establish a music scholarship program in honor of Isaac Gold. The idea had immediate acceptance, but had to be cleared with Isaac, who expressed no interest in having a big fuss made over his retirement. John's idea of scholarships won him over in the end.

The name J.T. Tyler was enough to guarantee a sell-out. John did not disappoint them, giving a two-and-a-half-hour concert to one standing ovation after another. As he returned to the stage for his third encore, he took the microphone and asked for quiet.

"Thank you all for such a rousing response. Every performer lives for nights like this. However, tonight we are here to honor a man who could have heard such responses in his life but chose to teach and not perform. What music we have missed because of that decision, we'll never know. However, it couldn't have been greater than the love of music he has instilled in thousands of students throughout the years. His influence on my life is well known to all of you. Isaac, you gave me a future of richness and beauty that I could have never otherwise known. Thank you. In my gratitude, I'm going to do what I did ten years ago in this room. I'll not make a speech, but instead sing a song that says what you have meant to me, Isaac."

Granddad Earl interjected at this point in his story of John, "I'll not give you the lessons of this story, Sean, because John did it perfectly when he sang."

I was young and kind of wild
You brought peace to this young child
I was young and needed guidance
You showed me how to take a chance

I was young and so unsure
Your kindness was so pure
So young and so uncertain
Acceptance lifts my burden

You gave me music
To light my way
You gave me music
That I could play

You gave me music
That was so rare
You gave me music
That I could share
And when I play I know you're there

I was young, how did you see
There was talent deep in me
I was young, how you did know
Someday music would flow

Now I'm older, and I got fame
Through it all, I stayed the same
Just a young boy that you could see
All the promise that I could be

You gave me music
To light my way
You gave me music
That I could play
You gave me music
That was so rare
You gave me music
That I could share
And when I play I know you're there

charlie

The heart of marriage is memories.

Bill Cosby

My favorite Christmas tale of Farrellville was introduced to me by Granddad on the Christmas Eve prior to my marriage to Kathy. It was about a man named Charlie.

Charlie stood in his basement, staring at the shelves, on which were stacked boxes and plastic bins filled with Christmas decorations. Every year, it seemed that Santa's elves had snuck in during the summer and added more boxes. He thought to himself, *I don't remember putting this many boxes down here last year.*

Christmas was his wife's favorite holiday. Mary couldn't pass a Christmas store or holiday craft show without check-

ing it out, which usually meant adding at least one deco-
ration to her collection. Fortunately, she was diligent in
labeling the contents of each box and bin when she packed
them at the end of the holiday season. Charlie surveyed her
handwriting on each label, which identified the contents
and the room in the house where they were to be placed.

"Where to start?" he asked himself. "Might as well
begin with the family room tree," he said as he pulled down
the large rectangular box. As he pulled it up the basement
steps, he thought, *I hope these lights work this year.* He had
spent hours last year checking lights to find the defective
ones that caused the entire string to go out.

He set the box down near the corner of the family
room, where the tree had resided for the last twenty-four
Christmases. Of course, when the boys were still living at
home, they bought a natural tree every year, because Mary
loved the fragrance that it gave the house. After the boys
left home, Charlie finally convinced her to buy an artificial
tree with lights, since it was much easier to put up and
take down. He pulled the sections out of the box, put them
together, and assembled the base. "The moment of truth,"
he said as he plugged lights into the wall outlet. Amazingly,
they all lit. "Well, Mary, that's a good omen."

Charlie brought up the trees for the bedroom and the
dining room. The dining room tree lit up the first time.
While the bedroom tree had one string out, Charlie was
able to find the culprit, and replaced that light with a fresh
bulb. He continued hauling the decorations up out of the
basement throughout the morning. He always considered himself the labor, while Mary was the decorator. She
decided where each piece went on the walls, the shelves,

and the counters. Somehow, she could always remember these locations from year to year, while Charlie couldn't remember from one day to another where he left his car keys. Room by room, he decorated the house, and as he finished that evening, he said, "How does it look, Mary? Not too bad, huh?"

"You did really well, Charlie. The house is beautiful!"

Late into the evening, Charlie sat in his easy chair, looking at the ornaments on the family room tree. Each had a history or story that took him back over the past Christmases that he and Mary had shared. He remembered their first tree after they were married. It couldn't have been more than four feet tall. To call it straggly would have been a compliment. For decorations, Mary had cut strips of colored paper and stapled them together to make a chain of loops that became the garland that draped the tree. She took used flash bulbs (*Yikes, who remembers flash bulbs these days,* he thought), dipped them in white glue and glitter, and attached them to the branches with pipe cleaners as the ornaments. A star made from aluminum foil topped her masterpiece. As he remembered it now, it was as glorious as the Christmas tree illuminated by the president on the White House lawn.

"That was a real masterpiece, Mary."

"Why thank you, Charlie."

His eyes went to a small picture frame ornament that said "Baby's First Christmas." The photo that he had taken of Connor in the hospital reflected in the tree light attached to the branch below. Little could one tell from that red puffy face, which vaguely resembled Richard Nixon (*Didn't all newborns resemble Nixon,* he thought), that he would become such a beautiful boy and handsome man. Conner, so gifted intellectually, physically, and emotionally, was all a parent could hope for.

He then found the second picture frame with another "Nixon" infant, Jack. Jack, whose entry into this life had been difficult, but true to his nature, he overcame this hardship with a deep breath and the longest and loudest cry the delivery room staff had ever heard. He left no doubt in anyone's mind that he was there to stay. His determined personality showed itself right at the beginning. Charlie remembered his and Mary's shock at the deformity of his left arm and leg. Their precious little boy wasn't perfect! *How shortsighted that initial reaction was,* he thought, for Jack had many qualities that weren't as apparent then but which became the source of great pride for Mary and him as Jack grew up.

Charlie's eye was attracted to a pair of shiny silver globes with a golden angel depicted on each of them. Mary had bought one for each of the boys and told them that they represented the guardian angels God had given them for protection and guidance. Each year, she hung the angel globes next to the picture frames to reinforce that image with the boys. Normally, boys of their age wouldn't take such things seriously, and that was the case with Connor and Jack until their cousin Angelina became ill. She told them of her glimpses of angels and her devotion to her guardian angel. They saw how her devotion gave her strength and courage right up to the last day. After that, they no longer made light of their mother's angel globes.

Another ornament attracted Charlie's attention and caused him to smile.

"Remember when you bought that one, Mary?"

"Yes, Charlie. At the time, you didn't think it was so funny."

The blue ornament had Santa standing in front of a sign with arrows that pointed in opposite directions; each labeled "North Pole." Santa was holding a road map, scratching his head, with a confused look on his face.

"I still say that I wasn't lost. I just wanted to see the countryside, Mary."

"Of course you did, Charlie."

Charlie couldn't really take his excuse seriously. He *was* lost. That trip had started out as a Sunday outing with the boys a couple of weeks before Christmas. Mary had read about a small town in the northern part of the state that had interesting antique and craft shops. These didn't particularly interest Charlie and the boys; however, the historical railroad station in the town had a small museum that they would enjoy, while Mary wandered through flotsam and jetsam of other people's lives that made up the bulk of goods found in most antique stores.

His downfall had been trying a shortcut that took them off the main highway and into a series of ever smaller country roads that finally led them to a small crossroads, consisting of a two-pump gas station, a small diner, and a general store. While the car didn't need fuel, the boys did. They entered the diner and sat in the nearest booth. The few diners at the counter turned toward them when they entered and recognized them as non-locals as Mary commented, "City folk lost in the country."

After the waitress gave them menus and took their orders, Charlie reluctantly asked where they were. Of course, her answer meant nothing to him since he had no idea where "here" was. Mary took up the inquiry by asking about their destination and was not surprised by the bemused expression of the waitress.

"Oh, I'm afraid that you're going in the wrong direction. You should have turned east about twenty miles ago."

Mary gave Charlie that "I told you so" look that he had seen all too often before. Bless her, though, she didn't say it in front of the boys. And yes, she had suggested that he needed to go east at least three times in the last thirty miles.

As the boys wolfed down their hamburger and fries, the general store caught Mary's eye.

"It's getting too late to get to that town this afternoon, Charlie. Why don't we look through that general store before we head home. I'm sure that there are some tools and things that will interest you and the boys, and I'll wander through the rest of the store."

Thus, the lost Santa ornament was discovered in one corner of the general store, where Christmas decorations were displayed. Charlie wasn't aware of the subject of her purchase until the next weekend, when the tree was brought home, placed, and decorated. There, right at the top in the front, was Santa scratching his head and perusing his map. Not wanting to give her the satisfaction, he never mentioned it. Each year, however, it always found its way to the top and front of the Christmas tree. And there it was again this year, in its favorite spot.

Charlie looked at an assortment of handmade ornaments, mostly crude and unsophisticated, that had been the products of Connor's and Jack's efforts in elementary school. Some were papier-mâché, and others were made from wire and glitter. Each in its own way was a natural successor to Mary's original flashbulb ornaments.

So many ornaments, so many years. They all seemed to flow over Charlie as a wave of images and memories: the miniature trophy that Mary had converted to an ornament the year Jack had been given the award for the Farrellville 10k Race; the sports ornaments reflecting Connor's achievements; the mortarboard caps with tiny tassels for the boys' college degrees; the frames with pictures of the boys with their wives (Connor and Rachael, Jack and Gail); and of course, the porcelain booties with the names and birthdates of the grandkids.

The last ornament, which Charlie had tried to avoid, was the one Mary had found last spring, the week she learned that she had cancer. As with the Santa, she hadn't told Charlie about it. He had only found it, tucked away, when he opened the ornament box this morning. The note attached said,

My dearest Charlie:

This will be my last ornament for our tree. If I am gone by Christmas, please decorate the house as we've always done. You know how I've always loved the Christmas season and wanted to share it with those I loved—you, the boys, and their families. Continue to share the festive spirit with them for me. I'll be here to help you one way or the other. Just talk to me, Charlie, and I'll hear

you. Remember that one day we'll be able to celebrate
Christmas together again. I'll be waiting.

Love,

Mary

Charlie held the ornament in his hand. It depicted Mary
and Joseph's journey to Bethlehem, where she would give
birth to the Christ Child. On it, Mary had written in black
ink, "God blessed two Marys with perfect husbands."

"I don't think so, Mary."

"Let me be the judge of that, Charlie," he could almost
hear her say.

ray

The greatest griefs are those we cause ourselves.

Sophocles

Granddad and I were having a conversation in his basement one day about how decisions we make can affect our life in unexpected ways. To illustrate the point, he gave me his last life lesson by telling me the story of a man, Ray Hunt, who had not grown up in Farrellville and wasn't even a resident. The lesson of the story was about life itself. When Granddad introduced us, Ray was standing under a large oak tree on a hillside overlooking Farrellville, but his story began on a train—a train that was bringing him to Farrellville.

Ray sat in the observation lounge car as the train wound through the narrow mountain pass. It was early morning in late October, and the rising sun illuminated the yellows and oranges of the foliage that adorned the steep slopes above the rolling river that followed the rails. The river reflected the clear blue sky that framed the color of the mountains. The rhythmic sound of the wheels on the rails and the undulation of the car held Ray in a trance-like contemplation. He was not ordinarily a contemplative man, but this trip somehow facilitated reflection. He hadn't thought much about why he had chosen the train over flying, but now he understood. Subconsciously, he had wanted the time to think about his life, both past and future, to sort things out, and to deal with issues that still remained unresolved.

He and Ginny were returning to Farrellville, her childhood home, after a long absence. He chastened himself for waiting so long to take her home. They had meant to come back sooner, but since the tragic death of her parents two years after Ray and Ginny were married, the primary reasons for returning seemed to have gone away. He wondered now whether bringing her back here, to a place that held so many happy memories, would have lessened the sadness that had consumed her over the years.

The train was to arrive this afternoon. Ray smiled, remembering his first vision of Farrellville, which reminded him of the Charles Wysocki prints that his grandmother had on the walls of her living room. The small farms and the colorful fields, the white clapboard houses on the edge of town, and the cluster of buildings in the downtown appeared from the train window to have been painted by the artist. Growing up in a large city, Ray had never spent time in a small town.

It was also in October, many years ago, when Ray stepped onto the platform, an eager young attorney from the largest law firm in the state capital, to represent a couple who were involved in a nasty dispute over their grandfather's estate, which included a sizable farm and various commercial properties in the county. No will existed at the time of the grandfather's death, but he had written letters to various family members, indicating to whom his property interests were to be given. Unfortunately, the letters conflicted, and several properties were not addressed, so Ray came to review the county records and research the property claims of his clients. Since he would be spending a couple of days there to complete his research, he would take the opportunity to talk to the locals about the grandfather and the other heirs who lived in the town. Possibly he could uncover something that would clarify the old man's intentions relative to his clients.

Standing on the station platform, he caught the scent of smoke that came from the chimneys in town. It was late afternoon, and the setting sun cast long shadows as it slowly descended behind the hills. He felt a chill from the wind that blew in from the west. A shower of red and yellow leaves rode on the breeze and gradually gave in to gravity's pull as they dropped to the ground. As he was about to ask for directions to the Farrellville Inn, where he would be spending the next two nights, he spotted it a block down the street from the station. *Well that's convenient,* he thought to himself as he picked up his bag and briefcase and walked out of shadow of the station into the sunshine.

The Farrellville Inn was a three-story brick building on a corner lot of Main Street. As he approached, he could see a small garden in the back, framed with maple trees that gave off a crimson glow in the receding sunlight. He could hear the sound of running water, which turned out to be a small but steady flowing stream at the rear of the garden. Standing at the bottom of the steps to the porch, Ray surveyed his residence for the next two nights. The lights were on inside, and as he started up the stairs the carriage lights on each side of the front door came on as if to welcome him. Illuminated, the building had a comforting and cozy aspect. Ray opened the door and entered. At the registration desk stood a short, stout, gray-haired woman who greeted him with a smile.

"Good afternoon … or evening now, I guess. Welcome to the Farrellville Inn. Are you Mr. Hunt?" she asked.

"Uh, why yes, I am. How did you know?"

"When your secretary made the reservation, she was very specific about the arrangements. She said that you would be arriving on the five-thirty train, that you would require a single room with a queen-size bed for two nights, and may require a rental car while in town. She also described you, but frankly, I don't think she did you justice," she concluded, with a twinkle in her eye.

"Well, yes. That does sound like Lillian. As for the description, she's seen enough of me to temper any initial impression that one might have."

"Mr. Hunt, I am Mrs. Wells, proprietor of the Farrellville Inn. I have reserved our best room for you," she said as she withdrew a brass key from the cabinet on the wall. She slid a registration card across the counter. "Please sign at the bottom; I've already filled it in based on the information provided by your ... Lillian."

Ray scrawled his signature and handed the card to Mrs. Wells, who filed it in the desk drawer.

"If you will follow me, I'll show you to your room," she said as she walked toward the staircase. "We have a new elevator in the rear, but if you don't mind, I prefer to show my rooms from the staircase. I think it has a more proper ambiance than going up in a metal box."

"That will be fine, Mrs. Wells," Ray said as he followed her upstairs.

"Your room is in the rear corner of the second floor, overlooking the garden and the stream. The sound of the water is very soothing. It will drown out the traffic noise from Main Street."

Ray almost told her that the activity he had seen on Main Street during his brief walk from the train certainly didn't come close to his definition of traffic. Accustomed to the cacophony of big cities, Ray had learned to sleep through more noise than a hundred Farrellvilles could generate. "I'm sure I'll sleep quite soundly here," he said instead.

Mrs. Wells inserted the key in the lock and opened the door to his room. Since the room was on the southwest corner of the inn, he could see the setting sun through the windows: two on the side wall, and two on the rear. The view of the garden and the sound of the stream confirmed Mrs. Wells's promise of tranquility. The room décor was a bit old fashioned for his taste, but was bright and cheerful. Most importantly, the bed looked very comfortable.

"This is a very nice room, Mrs. Wells. I'll be quite comfortable."

"The closet is that door, and the bathroom is behind this door," she said as she handed the key to him. "Our dining room is now serving dinner, and is open until ten p.m. Breakfast is served starting at five thirty in the morning. If you prefer room service, dial nine on that phone. If you need anything, please don't hesitate to call me. Just dial zero."

"Thank you, Mrs. Wells. You've made me feel most welcome."

His comment brought a smile and a slight blush to her face as she closed the door and descended the staircase.

Ray suddenly felt tired. It already had been a long couple of days. Taking three days away from the office meant that he had worked late the previous two nights and had risen at four thirty this morning to finish his work for another client before catching the train.

However, weariness was superseded by hunger, as he had only had coffee for breakfast and had delayed lunch until boarding the train, only to discover the dining car consisted of several vending machines dispensing soft drinks, candy, and unsatisfying, high-calorie snacks. Tempted to order room service, but afraid that he might fall asleep on that comfortable bed while waiting its delivery, Ray unpacked, went into the bathroom, washed his face in cold water, and, feeling somewhat refreshed, went downstairs to the dining room.

As he entered, an attractive young woman approached and asked, "Will someone be joining you for dinner?"

"Huh … oh … no. No one will be joining me. A table for one please," he stammered.

"Follow me," she said as she led him to a table by a window at the rear. Once again, he overlooked the garden and heard the sound of the stream. She handed him a menu. "My name is Ginny. I'll be serving you this evening. Would you like something to drink?"

"Uh, I think just water until I decide what to have," Ray replied as he tried not to stare at her. Something about her riveted his attention. He wasn't sure whether it was her eyes, green hazel with yellow flecks that shimmered in the low light of the room; her voice, which was as soft and soothing as the water in the stream; or her petite figure, which attracted every man in the room. He was captivated.

⁓⁓⁓

As Ray sat in the lounge car, the memory of his first encounter with Ginny still filled him with joy. He couldn't remember what he had ordered. He had a vague recollection that it was the evening special. What he did remember is that he ate and drank as much as possible, trying to stay as long as he could. He ordered several glasses of wine, several appetizers, a salad, an entree, dessert, and coffee. He'd order anything if it brought her back to his table. If she were aware of what he was doing, she didn't let on, although he did detect a bemused look after his second pot of coffee. When he could delay no further, primarily because his bladder was in revolution from the coffee infusion, he requested the check. He gave her a very generous tip, partly because he had been such a glutton, but mostly because he wanted to leave her with a positive impression of him.

That night fatigue finally overtook Ray, and he slept soundly. The alarm woke him at seven thirty the next morning, interrupting the last in a series of wonderful dreams that he had about a girl with green hazel eyes named Ginny.

He showered quickly, dressed, and rushed down to the dining room, hoping Ginny would be on the breakfast shift. He quickly scanned the room as he entered from the lobby. Two waitresses were serving; neither was Ginny. As one of the waitresses approached, he asked, "Is Ginny working this morning?"

"No, Ginny works the lunch and dinner shifts—not breakfast. Can I help you?"

"Uh, sure. Table for one," Ray said, trying to hide his disappointment.

Over breakfast, Ray adjusted his schedule for the day to allow lunch at the inn and a chance to see Ginny. After breakfast, he returned to his room and called the people on his list to arrange interviews that afternoon and the following day. He was successful in scheduling three that afternoon and another three the next morning. At nine a.m., he picked up the car that Mrs. Wells had reserved for him and visited the properties involved in the estate. He returned to the inn at one fifteen p.m. and headed right for the dining room. The lunch crowd had pretty much cleared out, so he had no difficulty in securing one of Ginny's tables. When she approached, he saw the same bemused look that she had had the previous evening.

"Hi, Ginny."

"Hi, Mr. Hunt."

"Please, call me Ray."

"Okay, Ray. Can I get you something to drink?"

"Sure, I'll have coffee."

"Coming right up," she said as she handed him a menu and returned to the kitchen.

While he didn't take as much time with lunch as with dinner last night, he did engage her in conversation. Since there were no customers at her other tables, she seemed pleased to talk to him. He told her about his business in town and his desire to talk to as many people as possible. She gave him names of people who weren't on his list and told him about the people he would interview that afternoon. Since she had been born and raised in Farrellville, she was a real source of information for his case. He learned that she had been working at the inn for four years while taking classes in the morning at the local community college. With the money she had earned to supplement her scholarship from a small private university, she planned to move to the state capitol next fall. He offered to engage her as an informal consultant to assist him with his research and to provide introductions to the people she had recommended to him. While she wasn't sure that she wanted to get involved, the hourly fee he proposed did interest her. He suggested that she think it over, and they could discuss it further when he returned for dinner that evening. After paying the check with another generous tip, he returned to his room to prepare for the afternoon's interviews.

He reviewed the brief biographies of the interviewees and the notes he had taken of Ginny's comments. Prior to leaving, he called his office and told Lillian that he would be extending his stay in Farrellville to interview the additional people recommended by Ginny.

"I'll inform Mr. Ferguson that you won't be back in the office until Monday."

"That's good, Lillian. I may stay through Saturday and return on the Sunday train,"

"Would you like me to rebook your ticket?"

"No thanks, Lillian. The station is only a block from the inn, so I'll take care of it myself."

"Very well, Mr. Hunt. Is there anything else I can do for you?"

"I can't think of anything right now. By the way, your choice of the inn was great. They gave me the best room in the place. Also, the dining room is excellent, with wonderful service."

"Mrs. Wells was very helpful. Did she get you a car?"

"Yes, I used it today to survey the properties."

"You have a nice weekend, and I'll see you on Monday."

"I plan to, Lillian. See you Monday."

The three interviews that afternoon confirmed the conflicts in the letters. The last interview, however, did clarify a couple of the property claims. As Ray drove back to town, he was hopeful that tomorrow's meetings would further clarify the case. Before returning to the inn, he stopped and exchanged his ticket. He was now booked on the eleven a.m. train on Sunday.

Once in his room, he changed from his lawyer's costume (blue suit, starched white shirt, dark tie, and polished dress shoes) into his casual clothes (khaki pants, white golf shirt, and loafers). As he entered the dining room, he again scanned it for Ginny, and immediately saw her smiling back at him as she crossed the room.

"Good evening, Mr. Hunt. May I show you to your table?"

"Well, first, call me Ray, and second, I didn't know I had a table reserved," he said with a smile.

"Oh yes…uh, Ray. All of our resident guests have reserved tables. Mrs. Wells insists."

"I wasn't informed of this benefit, but I am very pleased to take advantage of it. But may I ask who the server will be for that table this evening?"

"Why I am, of course. I requested it and hope you don't mind."

"Not at all, I have been most pleased with your service."

They resumed their conversation exactly where it had concluded at lunch. She had considered his consulting offer and accepted. Since she had Friday and Saturday off, she could accompany him on the additional interviews. He was delighted.

❦

As Ray recalled that dinner, it was then that he realized he wanted to spend the rest of his life with Ginny. She told him several years later that she felt the same thing that evening in the dining room.

Ginny turned out to be a great assistance to him over the next two days. One of the people she had recommended later became the key witness in settling the claims for his clients. On Saturday, following the last interview, Ray and Ginny spent the afternoon just walking downtown, sitting in the park under the clock tower, and having dinner at a roadhouse out in the county. Saturday night at the roadhouse featured a local band that played country music. City-boy Ray learned the two-step and danced the night away to fiddle and guitar music.

Over the next few months, while the estate was being

probated, Ray found many reasons to visit Farrellville. Some visits were business related, but most were personal. Ray met Ginny's parents and her younger sister, Rita. Fortunately, they seemed to take to Ray, and before long, he was made to feel part of the family. Ginny started at the university in August and lived in a small off-campus apartment with two other girls. Working with Ray convinced her to pursue a law degree upon graduation. Ginny was a quick study and had a fierce determination to succeed. She and Ray shared that determination and often spoke of one day forming their own firm.

Two years later and a month after graduation, Ginny and Ray were married. His career was advancing in the firm, and a partnership seemed to be visible on the horizon, that is, if you had a really strong telescope. With Ginny in law school and Ray climbing the corporate ladder, their lives were consumed with their careers. However, they always reserved time on Sunday afternoons to decompress and spend time to together, often short drives to the countryside, bike rides in the park, or discovering out-of-the-way pubs or restaurants.

They made only two trips to Farrellville while Ginny was in law school. The first trip was for Rita's wedding to a local boy that she had known since the first grade. After the wedding, the newlyweds moved to Detroit, where Ginny's new brother-in-law was starting his career with one of the big three automakers. The second trip was for her parents' funeral. They had been returning from spending Thanksgiving with Rita in Detroit, when a sudden ice storm hit them on the highway. Eyewitness accounts told of the car going out of control and hitting a bridge abutment. On a cold, rainy morning in December, Ginny and Rita buried their parents at the Farrellville cemetery. Ginny returned to Farrellville twice more, to settle her parents' estate and sell the family home.

The sun shone over the mountains as midmorning arrived. Ray returned to the lounge car with coffee and some sort of version of a Danish pastry that had been dispensed by the vending machine. Two small bites of the Danish confirmed Ray's opinion that it had a longer shelf life than the army's MRE (Meals Ready to Eat). He set the pastry aside and blew on his coffee. At least it was strong and hot.

Where had the years gone? Work, of course; there were always new clients and cases to be handled, battles to be won, and the climb up the ladder to a partnership. It all seemed so important at the time. But now, in retrospect, it wasn't that important at all.

Following the funeral, Ginny attempted to bury herself in completing law school and interviewing for jobs. She was a natural. She had a quick mind, a competitive spirit, and a passion for the law. Instead of joining Ray in his firm, she chose to join the county prosecutor's office. She said that it was her call to public service. In those years, more than a few defendants wished that her call had been toward other services, like nursing or teaching. Her conviction rate was the highest in the office. Eventually, she got the toughest and usually highest profile cases.

While they had talked of having a family, the time never seemed right. First, it was law school for her, and his workload to convince the partners of his value. Then it became her caseload with the prosecutor's office and his need to press just two more years to secure a partnership. But life is not subject to definitive plans, no matter how well conceived. Ray learned this one cold Monday morning, as he dressed in his lawyer costume to start another week. Ginny walked out of the bathroom with a sly grin and said, "Sit down, Ray, I need to tell you something."

"Sit down? What for?"

"I think you need to take this news sitting down, okay?"

Sitting, Ray said, "All right, I'm down and have now taken the perfect crease out of my pants. This will earn me ten demerits with the fashion enforcers at the office."

"Ray, I think I'm pregnant."

"Are you sure?"

"Well, pretty sure."

"When … uh … how, I mean, you are?"

"I think so," she said. "How do you feel about it?"

Of course, they had talked about kids, but it always seemed to be something for the future. But now it was real! A thousand thoughts and a million questions clouded his mind. *Me, a father? Am I ready for this now?*

All he could say was, "Uh, good. I think I feel pretty good about it. How about you?"

"I feel pretty good too. But I'm worried. Do you think we're ready to be parents?"

Ray came to her and wrapped his arms around her. "Sure. I think we can handle it. You'll make a great mother."

In the days that followed, Ray struggled to become comfortable with the image of himself as a father. While he could readily see Ginny as a good mother, just like her own, he still wondered if he had what it took. His own father had been a poor example. A drunkard who could not hold a job, his father abandoned the family when Ray was twelve years old. His mother had tried to soften the blow by telling Ray and his younger brother, Sam, that their father had taken a job in another state and would be back to take the family with him in a few months. Ray was old enough to sense the fabrication of the story, and besides, he wasn't sure his wanted the old man to return anyway. From that day on, Ray had to be the man of family. His mother worked two jobs to support the boys. For their part, Ray and Sam mowed lawns, ran errands, and generally picked up any odd jobs that boys of their age could be paid for. On the day he turned eighteen, three days after graduating high school, Ray enlisted in the army. He sent most of this pay home to his mother. The army taught him discipline and a trade, vehicle maintenance, which he was able to use to put himself through college and law school after his active service. Of course, the money that the army gave him for college was a big help as well.

A week after her announcement, Ginny received confirmation from the doctor's office of her pregnancy. Ray had not seen her really happy since her parents were alive. As they started a new plan, one that included the baby, Ginny and Ray discussed names. She wanted Ray for a boy's name, but he would not hear of it. He had never liked his name or his brother's for that matter. Ray and Sam seemed to be old-man names; indeed, Ray had been named for his father. Who wanted to call a baby boy Ray? No, Ray wanted a name that was good for a young boy as well as a man, even an old man. One of Ray's best childhood friends was named Danny, which seemed to Ray to be a perfect name—Danny as a boy, and Daniel as a man. So he convinced Ginny that a boy should be named Daniel. He also convinced her that a girl should be Virginia so she could be called Ginny—just like her mom.

Once again, life disrupted their perfect plan. At fourteen weeks, Ginny had the amniocentesis test, the results of which indicated that the baby had Down syndrome. The doctor also indicated that it was likely a boy. The doctor explained that the condition was a problem with the baby's chromosomes. Typically, it was the result of having an extra chromosome, forty-seven instead of the normal forty-six.

"What caused it?" Ginny asked. "Did I do something wrong?"

"We really don't know. And you didn't do something wrong. Normally, women over thirty-five are at greater risk, but that doesn't apply to you."

"I've seen Down syndrome children," Ray said. "Do they all have the same appearance?"

"Generally, yes," the doctor said. "Most people notice the slanting eyes, the flat face, and the small ears. But they also have shorter necks, arms, and legs. They can also be afflicted with breathing, heart, and ear problems."

"Do they have normal intelligence?" Ray asked.

"Generally below average, although they can usually get by with special care and support, depending on the severity of the condition."

"Can you tell how bad the baby's condition is?" Ginny asked.

"I'm afraid we can't determine that until birth, and then it may be a while before we really know."

"How about its life span?" Ray asked.

"It's shorter than normal, again, depending on the

severity. I know this is a shock to you, but it is important that you have this information. I want you to know that you have options available at this time."

"You mean treatment options?" Ginny asked.

"Yes, of course. But I must also inform you that you have another option concerning continuing with the pregnancy."

Ray took another sip of his coffee as the train rattled over a bridge, which spanned the river that they had been following for the past few hours. The noise and vibration reminded him of the jolt he had received from those words from the doctor. "Another option concerning continuing with the pregnancy," he had said. That option had not occurred to him, or Ginny, for that matter.

Ray looked over at the next lounge seat. There was Danny with his placid smile. How he wished he could have such a peaceful frame of mind. While Danny did not speak, Ray was sure he knew his thoughts and empathized with him. It seemed to Ray that Danny's simplicity and goodness were meant to offset the pain and sadness both he and Ginny carried these many years.

Danny's slanted eyes looked back at him. The flat features and the small ears were as the doctor had described them. But the doctor had not talked of the understanding and love that such a simple countenance could convey. He was thankful that Danny was with them as they returned to Farrellville.

While the accident that took Ginny's parents had been a shock, the true sadness didn't really enter their lives until that day in the doctor's office. It stayed with them in the years that followed. Ginny became pregnant two more times. Both ended in miscarriages. A few years later, after the hysterectomy to combat the cancer in her uterus, they realized that there would be no more pregnancies. Life indeed had taken their plans and thrown them asunder. Ray could see Ginny growing sadder, almost to despair. He tried to lift her spirits, but it was a false attempt because his own despondency weighed him down. He felt, no, he knew that he had failed her. She never accused him or rejected him but continued in her own sad way to love him.

Ray believed that he had followed in his father's footsteps, only in a different way. He didn't abandon his wife and home, but he wasn't there for her when she really needed him.

"Farrellville in twenty minutes … Farrellville is our next stop," announced the conductor. Ray snapped back to the present. He rose from his chair and headed back to his compartment to pack his bag and prepare for arrival.

Ray surveyed Farrellville as the train pulled into the station. It had grown significantly since his first visit. The downtown had expanded up and out. But he could still see the remnants of the Wysocki painting. The inn was still there, although in an expanded version. Mrs. Wells had left the inn to her children when she died, but they had quickly sold out to a regional hotel chain shortly thereafter. Ray thought it was probably for the best since what he had known of her children led him to believe that it would have been run into the ground under their direction. He would lay even odds that they had probably already gone through the money they received.

Ray dismounted the train and with bag in hand walked toward the baggage car.

As he approached, he took out the ticket voucher and handed it to the baggage clerk.

"Thank you, Mr. Hunt. If you'll wait over there on the platform, we'll have it out for you in just a minute."

Well, Ginny, you're finally home. Maybe you can finally find your peace here, Ray thought as he saw her casket emerge from the baggage car and placed on the wagon.

"If you can hold it here, I'll check inside to see if the funeral home hearse has arrived," Ray said to the clerk.

Just then, Ray saw the hearse drive up and the funeral director, Tom Watkins, open the passenger door.

"There they are now," Ray said.

"Hello, Ray," Watkins said. Turning to the clerk, he said, "My assistant will help you with the casket."

Ray shook Watkins's hand, "Hello, Tom. It's good to see you again."

"Everyone in town was saddened by Ginny's passing. I think we'll have a large crowd at the viewing this evening."

Only a viewing and burial would be held in Farrellville, since the formal funeral had been held two days before in the capitol city, where Ginny and Ray had spent their lives together.

"Thanks, Tom. She would have liked that. Have Rita and her family arrived yet?"

"Yes, they drove in last night. I believe they'll have the rooms adjoining yours at the inn."

"Great. I'll go check in at the inn."

"Fine, Ray. We'll have everything ready for you at six thirty."

"Thanks, Tom. I'll see you then."

Ray walked to the inn. Not seeing Mrs. Wells at the registration desk made the place a little less welcoming. After checking in and retiring to his room, he contacted Rita and arranged to meet them for an early dinner in the dining room at five p.m.

Entering the dining room at 4:55, Ray couldn't help but search for Ginny to see which table was hers. For a moment, he was startled to see her across the room, only to realize that it was Rita waving to him from a table near the rear window, the same table where he had first met Ginny. He crossed the room and gave Rita a hug. "How was your drive over yesterday?" he asked.

"It seemed longer than I remembered the trip. But it was a lot shorter than coming from Detroit. The funeral was very nice. I wanted to tell you that at the church, but the kids were so upset that we had to take them back to hotel. Frankly, I wasn't doing so well either. Thank God I had Roger. He has been my rock through all of this."

"I know, Rita. I don't know how I would have handled it without you guys."

"Ray, I know I've told you this before, but you can't keep blaming yourself. Ginny never did. She was part of the decision too," Rita said.

"Thanks, Rita, but it is something I can't forget or forgive myself for."

"You've got to forgive yourself, Ray. Let Ginny intercede for you. She has God's ear now."

"I'll try. I promise."

"I'm holding you to that promise," Rita said as she gave him another hug.

"Where are Roger and the girls?" Ray asked as they sat down.

"He's taking them to McDonald's for some comfort food. I don't think they'll make it to the viewing. They'll probably watch one of their videos tonight."

During dinner, Rita talked of the good times, especially the childhood years growing up in Farrellville. She told him about how excited Ginny was when she first met Ray and he offered her the consulting job. It was that experience that convinced Ginny to become a lawyer. After dinner Ray and Rita walked to the Watkins Funeral Home, which was two blocks west on Main Street. It was a clear, crisp fall evening with no clouds to blot out the bright canopy of stars.

❧❧❧

Ray remembered a similar night just a year ago when he and Ginny had walked through the park trying to cope with the news the doctor had given them that afternoon.

"The cancer is back," he had said solemnly.

Ginny had suspected as much, since she had begun feeling poorly a month before.

She hadn't said anything to Ray, but he had picked up on the little indications that he had seen in her first bout. He had gone with her the previous week to have the tests and again that day to get the results. He had never been one who prayed much, but that week he found himself seeking God's intervention all day, every day. He couldn't blame God for not hearing him since he had spoken so little to him in the past. Maybe God was telling him that life's decisions had consequences. When he expressed this thought to Ginny, she gently rebuked him, telling him that God doesn't hold grudges.

"I wish he would let me know that somehow," Ray said.

Last year was the longest of his life. He prayed for Ginny's recovery as she endured the terrible treatments that seemed only to deplete her strength. While there were moments for optimism, a gradual decline appeared inevitable. He also hoped for a sign from God that would allow him to overcome the guilt he felt. None had been forthcoming.

꙳

Ray knew that Ginny had many friends in Farrellville, but he was still overcome by the outpouring of affection from the many that filled the funeral home that evening. He certainly understood better now Ginny's request to be brought back here. This would be where he would want to be also, since it had been more of a home to him than anywhere else.

The clear night gave way to a bright, sunny morning. A gentle breeze blew in from the west, putting an additional chill in the air. As Ray stepped from the car, he pulled up the collar of his overcoat. He saw Rita, Roger, and the girls emerge from their car and walk toward the gravesite.

The cemetery was located on a hill overlooking Farrellville. To the north was downtown, laid out in rectilinear patterns. The view to the south and east was of farmland, like a large quilt made by Mother Nature. To the west, the residential areas extended to the foothills of the range that crossed the state, north to south. Ray had been here once before, in this very spot, for the burial of Ginny's parents. Now this would be the final resting place for Ginny and someday for him. The gravesites were next to a large oak tree, whose branches offered shelter to those that lay beneath.

The crowd was not as large as last night because another burial was being held on the other side of the cemetery. It was a short ceremony. Afterwards, as the crowd returned to their cars, Ray stood silently with his hand on the casket.

"You were right, Ginny. I needed to seek forgiveness before I could expect a sign from God. Well, I'm trying to learn to forgive myself, but I'll never forget."

Ray looked up and smiled at Danny standing by the casket. Danny returned the smile in his gentle, simple way.

"Danny, when you came to me the night Ginny died, I realized that you were God's messenger—the sign. You let me know that Ginny was all right and that God was listening."

Danny never saw life because of the decision that had been made when Ray finally convinced Ginny that termination of the pregnancy would be better for all of them. Danny would not have to lead a life of suffering with abnormality. Ginny would not be held down by a life of caregiving, which would reduce her quality of life. Finally, and ultimately the most selfish reason, Ray would not have to deal with fatherhood at a time when he wasn't really ready. "Besides," he had told Ginny, "we can have more children when we're ready. When we can plan for them."

As Ray turned from the casket to return to the car, he

looked back at Danny, still standing at the grave. He raised his right hand and gave Ray a final farewell wave.

Approaching Tom, who was standing next to the hearse, Ray noticed the large crowd at the other burial.

"You had another burial today, Tom?"

"Yes, it was a very sad case," Tom replied. "A young mother was killed last week while driving a school bus. The morning train derailed and would have struck the bus, if Rebecca—that was her name—hadn't reacted quickly to avoid the collision. The bus went down the embankment, hit a tree, and turned over into the river."

"Were any of the children killed?" Ray asked.

"No," Tom said, "fortunately a boy walking to school saw the bus in the river, rushed to break the windows, and got the kids out in time."

"Wow! He sounds like a brave young man."

"Yeah, but what's so amazing is that he was the last person you would expect it from."

"Why," Ray asked.

"Well, he wasn't quite normal, if you know what I mean. People thought he was kind of slow and simple, you see."

Ray immediately thought of Danny. "What is his name, Tom?"

Tom replied, "His name is Daniel."

epilogue

As I reminisce about my days and years in Farrellville, I am interrupted by Kathy, who has brought our two-year-old son down here into Granddad's basement.

"Sean, I brought Stevie down so you could introduce him to Farrellville."

As he reached the bottom of the stairs, his face lit up when he saw stretched out before him Granddad's model train layout of Farrellville. Each building, street, hillside, stream, and plastic figure in the town was just as it was when Granddad constructed them on that plywood platform decades before. The trains that ran throughout the miniature world that was Farrellville brought joy to Stevie's eyes and tears to mine.

I hoped that each plastic figure that Granddad had carefully placed in the town, and had introduced to me long ago through his stories of their lives and the lessons they taught, would become as real to Stevie.

"Stevie, come and sit on my lap. I want to introduce you to an old friend of mine."

I picked up the figure of a seated man who, with his brightly painted blue pants, red shirt, and brown fedora, was the same as when Granddad introduced us long ago.

"Daniel, this is my son, Stevie. Stevie, this is Daniel."

Stevie smiled and said, "Hi, Daniel!"

"Now close your eyes for just a second, Stevie, while I put Daniel back in Farrellville."

With his eyes tightly shut, I placed the small figure on the little bench in the park.

"Open your eyes, Stevie. Where's Daniel?"

author biography

G.E. Brock became an author after a successful career in real estate development in two of the largest and most successful planned communities in America (Irvine, California, and Columbia, Maryland). However, his primary vocation is as a father of four daughters and grandfather of twelve grandchildren, who provide the inspiration and source for the stories he tells. He lives in Virginia with his wife, Kathleen.

listen|imagine|view|experience

AUDIO BOOK DOWNLOAD INCLUDED WITH THIS BOOK!

In your hands you hold a complete digital entertainment package. Besides purchasing the paper version of this book, this book includes a free download of the audio version of this book. Simply use the code listed below when visiting our website. Once downloaded to your computer, you can listen to the book through your computer's speakers, burn it to an audio CD or save the file to your portable music device (such as Apple's popular iPod) and listen on the go!

How to get your free audio book digital download:

1. Visit www.tatepublishing.com and click on the e|LIVE logo on the home page.
2. Enter the following coupon code:
   1275-c51b-047a-c143-a8ca-f1c5-d0a9-c394
3. Download the audio book from your e|LIVE digital locker and begin enjoying your new digital entertainment package today!